Sophisticated Ladies

By the same author

BOWIE
PILGRIMS

Sophisticated Ladies

Gerard Mac

Gerard Mac

New Millennium

292 Kennington Road, London SE11 4LD

British Library in publication data.
A catalogue record for this book is
obtainable from The British Library.

Printed and bound by Watkiss Studios Ltd.
Biggleswade, Beds.
Issued by New Millennium*
Set in 12 point Times New Roman Typeface
ISBN 1 85845 248 1

* An imprint of The Professional Authors' & Publishers' Association

"One more drink and I'd have been
under the host."
Dorothy Parker (1893-1967)

Chapter One

She had delayed coming back to the house for as long as she reasonably could but they were still there, gossiping in hushed voices and rattling her teacups. They were always the same, never missed a trick or a good funeral. Sombre in black with black hats exhumed from the depths of wardrobes these inveterate mourners hovered in hunched groups or perched on the edges of armchairs. It was an unkind thought, Paula knew, but just then she couldn't help thinking they were like vultures, picking over the remains of a sausage roll or whatever was left of a person's life. Most of them she only ever saw on occasions such as this.

Rose caught her eye then handed her a cup of coffee with a whispered, "Shall I tell 'em all to bugger off?"

Ted had died on the Friday night and though it broke her heart to feel his hand go limp in hers she was glad he'd gone. He'd suffered enough and, after all, the only one it really mattered to was her. The children were grown up now and though they both loved their Dad and had always loved him they had their own lives to lead.

The mourners had nodded their drooping heads. It was just as well, wasn't it? they said. It was for the best. And Paula had nodded back, thinking: No! It wasn't! It wasn't for the best! He was my husband, the father of my children and he's dead and I'm here, all alone.

An abrasive old aunt, bent almost double by osteoporosis, tripped over a fireside rug, staggered sideways then stepped back to right herself.

"Mad cow disease," murmured Rose.

Rose was Paula's cleaner. She had volunteered to stay without pay at the house on the morning of the funeral, help with the buffet et cetera and hand out cups of tea. And she stayed behind now to help with the washing up.

Paula's two daughters thought she was mad to employ Rose. With hoots of derision and some exaggeration they told how she cleaned the house before Rose came then cleaned up in the kitchen after Rose left. Why do you do it? they asked. Because I like her, Paula always replied, and she makes me laugh.

Rose came for a couple of hours twice a week and invariably stayed all morning, chattering her way through two pots of tea and smoking cigarettes. She apologised constantly for the smoke and was always on the verge of giving up. In fact, every night before she went to sleep she would ask for the help and support of a god she professed not to believe in. 'Please, God,' she would say aloud, 'let me stop smoking.' And before breakfast she would start again.

"You'll miss him, y'know," she said, when they'd all gone.

Paula paused, her gloved hands in the washing up water. "What was it like? I mean, when Mr Parker died."

"Well," Rose said, lighting another cigarette, "it was odd at first. Sort of unreal. I never thought I'd miss him. But I did. He was away all week and he only came home at weekends. He'd be in the pub till about three most Sundays and he'd come home roaring drunk. I could always hear him coming. He never used the lift, 'cos we're only on the first floor, and I'd hear him coming up the stairs singing and shouting, 'Yo ho ho! And a bottle of rum!' "

She laughed. "He'd kick off his trousers and he'd run round the bedroom shouting, 'Where are yer, me ol' beauty? I got a present for yer!' And I'd manage to lock myself in the bathroom."

"Oh, Rose!" Paula said reprovingly, but trying not to laugh aloud.

"I'd call out, 'Shan't be a minute, my love. Get yourself undressed and lie on the bed.' And he'd call back, in his Cockney accent, 'Right y'are, me ocean queen!' "

"Was he a seaman then - Mr Parker?"

"A seaman?" Rose looked blank. "No, no. He was a long distance lorry driver."

"Oh," Paula said, none the wiser.

"I think he went on the Broads once," Rose offered. "On holiday."

"So what happened on these Sunday afternoons?"

"Not a lot." Rose laughed. "I'd wash my hair and run my bath and by the time I came out he'd be sleeping like a baby. He wouldn't remember whether we'd done owt or not." She smiled. "He'd wake up at four o'clock ready for his dinner and his favourite programme on the radio. 'Sing Something Sinful,' he used to call it."

"I think Phil's here," Paula said, at the window.

Phil was Rose's one and only son, a used car dealer. He always seemed to be road testing some vehicle and he would often pick up his mother from Paula's in a shiny new car. In a rough and ready way he was not bad-looking and with his little black moustache and his cheeky grin his mission in life seemed to be to charm the ladies, all ladies, even his mother who thought he was wonderful anyway.

"You'll be all right," Rose said, finding her coat.

"I don't know," Paula said. "It's not so much the thought of being alone. It's the thought of growing old alone."

"Of growing old at all," Rose asserted. "Did you see that old dear in the corner?"

"Ted's Aunt Em."

"Must be ninety if she's a day. She's stone deaf and she can't stop her hands shaking. She was rattling her cup in her saucer as if she was doing a rumba. Bloody tea was all over the place."

"I'd hate to get like that," Paula said.

"You've got to watch it, Paula. Make sure you don't. If there's no fella there when you're getting undressed it's easy to let things go. Believe me, I know."

"Well, you're in pretty good shape."

"I have to work at it and so will you from now on. That's why you're going to come to Keep Fit with me every Tuesday. If you don't you'll find your boobs start to droop, then your chest caves in and when you look round it's sticking out of your back. Before you know it you've got the hump."

"I'm getting the hump just listening to this."

"Words of warning, my love. That's all. You've got to keep on your toes. I do and I reckon when I start to lose the battle, when they start to talk over my head - you know how they do. 'How is she today? She all right? Shame, isn't it?' Then that'll be it. Two bottles of Gin and a gobful of Paracetamols. That'll be me."

"What a prospect!"

"Oh, you're all right, girl. Plenty of time yet. As our

Phil said just this morning, you're not exactly an old banger, are you? He reckons there's plenty of mileage left on your clock."

You must go to the Solicitors', Ted had said. If anything happens to me, if I suddenly pop off or something, go and see Jim Ponsonby. Her appointment was for ten thirty and it was only ten fifteen. Punctuality had never been one of Paula's virtues but now she was alone in the world she was surprised to find she was early.

Ponsonby and Pryke was an old-established family firm. Been in the business for four generations. Their discreet little office in the town centre had survived the redevelopment mania of the seventies and was still intact in a cobbled backwater close to the garish outlets of the multiples in the already run down and tatty new shopping precinct. Ponsonby and Prykes' only concession to modernisation was a mock-Georgian window in white and a black front door with shiny brass furnishings from Knobs and Knockers.

The brass plate between the door and the window had been forgotten in the update. It was dingy now, tinged green with the mildew of the years like the firm's senior partner, Aloysius Pryke, who was so vague and useless everyone was pleased and relieved when he didn't come in. Whenever it caught his eye Jim Ponsonby, the firm's dashing though not so young live wire, resolved to have the brass plate polished. But he never did. He also resolved to find a way to oust Aloysius. But he never did that either.

Paula took a seat in Reception - three second-hand dining chairs and a battered coffee table strewn with old copies of *Country Life* and *Yachts and Yachting*, the magazines courtesy of Mr Pryke who once kept a small boat on Windermere. She found herself facing a young woman with frizzed-out, ginger hair, a skimpy scarlet top open to the fourth button and a very tight, very short, off-white mini skirt.

"Like the bleedin' dentist's in 'ere, init?" the young woman said, lighting a cigarette.

"We don't allow smokin' in the office," the baby-faced blonde at the switchboard announced in a querulous high-pitched trill.

"Is that a fact?" the young woman responded and she puffed out a great billowing cloud of smoke.

The little blonde pouted her lips with a glance at Paula that said: You try to do your job and that's what you get. Then a buzzer went and she stood up. With her nose in the air, as if the young woman no longer existed, she said primly in her receptionist's voice, "Will you come this way, please, Mrs Blossom?"

A spotty young man in spectacles, a stiff three-piece suit and an even stiffer white collar stood up behind his desk, a little surprised as Paula entered his office. "Take a seat," he invited in a sudden falsetto. Then, attempting to bring his voice under control, he added in a forced baritone, "Please!"

Paula sat facing him across his desk. She felt sorry for him. He'd cut himself shaving that morning and a small square of toilet paper had been stuck to his chin to stem the flow and promptly forgotten. He still hadn't won his long drawn out battle with acne and he was clearly self-conscious, unsure of how he should play his newly acquired role of legal executive.

Behind the young man, above an empty fireplace, was a large canvas, a portrait of the firm's founder,

Angus H. Ponsonby. In a high wing collar he looked down with disdain, as if he totally disapproved of this latest edition to his august enterprise. Nervously the young man picked up the folder before him.

Paula presumed Jim Ponsonby had been delayed. Perhaps she should make a new appointment, come back at a more convenient time. She had only come along for a private chat with a friend of her husband. That was all. Not to discuss anything specific. But she didn't want to hurt the young man's feelings.

He coughed, adjusted his thick-lensed spectacles and looked over the top of the folder. "Were you drunk at the time?"

"Sorry?" Paula said.

Shrinking back a little into his stiff collar he asked, "Had you had too much to drink?"

Jim Ponsonby put his head round the door, eyes alight in welcome. "Paula! Sorry I'm late." To the young man he said, "There's been a bit of a mix-up, Nigel. Mrs Blossom is mine. I'm afraid you've got the wrong client."

Nigel blushed a bright red and the dried out piece of toilet paper fluttered down from his chin and landed on the desk. Surreptitiously, or so he thought, he covered it with the folder. "I don't know how this can happen. It's all perfectly clear." He stared tragically at Paula. "All the girl has to do is put a sticker against each client's name in the book. My stickers are blue. Mr Ponsonby's stickers are pink."

"Yes, yes, Nigel," Jim Ponsonby said. "I think Sharon must have got her stickers in a twist."

He whisked Paula away and ushered her into his own, rather better appointed office. "Cup of coffee for

Mrs Blossom, please, Sharon," he called as they passed through Reception. "She got you mixed up with the girl in the mini," he said, lowering his voice, and he held her chair as she sat down. "Sorry about that."

"What has she done."

"Who?"

"The girl in the mini."

"Oh." Jim Ponsonby smiled. "Bit of a character, it seems. She's come in for a consultation. From what I can gather she has a penchant for pouring pints of beer into policemen's hats."

Paula laughed.

His eyes softened. "I'm glad to see you can still laugh."

She nodded. "I don't think Ted would want me to go around feeling sorry for myself."

Sharon came in with two cups of coffee on a tray. "Sorry about that, Mr Ponsonby. I was sure Nigel's thingies were pink."

"How much did they charge yer?" It was the girl in the mini skirt and before Paula could reply she went on, "Charged me a fiver. A fiver for 'arf an 'our. Twenty minutes really. You'll be more, I expect. You got a coffee."

By accident they had met outside Marks and Spencer.

"Do yer know what 'e said?"

"Who?" Paula asked politely.

"Little Spotted Dick in there. He said if I 'ave to go to court I shouldn't wear me skirt so short. Gives 'em the wrong idea."

"Oh, I don't know," Paula said. "Not everyone can wear a mini. I certainly can't. Haven't got the legs. But you have. You have very good legs."

"Yer nice you, aren't yer?" the girl responded. And then: "Hey, I could murder a drink!"

"Well, to be honest," Paula said, "the coffee in there was awful. And it was cold. Let me buy you one."

"A coffee? No, I mean a proper drink. Come on, there's a nice little pub just 'ere."

Paula hesitated. "I don't usually go in pubs."

"Come on," the girl insisted. "Hair down, skirts up. That's what me granma used to say."

Paula laughed and followed her new found friend into the White Lion.

"The name's Terry, by the way."

"Er ... Paula," Paula reciprocated.

"That's nice. Sort o' posh, init? My name's Theresa, really, but me husband said it sounds too much like a bloody saint for me. It was 'im what started calling me Terry."

They found a table in a quiet corner.

"I'd like to buy the drinks, if I may," Paula said, "but I'm a bit shy about going up to the bar." She pressed a five pound note into Terry's hand. "Would you mind?"

"No problem," Terry said and she was back with a dry sherry and a Bacardi and coke almost before Paula's eyes had grown accustomed to the midday gloom.

Terry shook her frizzed-out hair towards the bar. "Look at 'im! Didn't come into 'is office 'til gone ten."

One foot on the rail, Jim Ponsonby was chatting amiably with two other men.

"That's the one you saw."

"Mr Ponsonby," Paula confirmed.

Terry made a noise in her throat. "Ponsonby and Prick."

Paula was about to say it's pronounced Pryke as in bike, but Terry went on, "He's a ponce an' I expect the other one's a prick."

"He's quite nice really," Paula said.

"You like everyone, don't yer? Now me, I always seem to get on the wrong side of people. Wrong side of the law an' all."

Paula wanted to ask but she didn't. She felt sure Terry was going to tell her anyway.

"It's me 'usband," Terry said. "He can be a right bastard. He 'as this silly little bitch 'e sees every Friday night. They work in the same office. He's been 'aving it off with 'er for ages."

"Shame," Paula said quietly.

"Oh, I don't mind that. Keeps 'im out o' mischief. At least, I know where 'e is. An' she doesn't cost 'im much. She's one o' these liberated women. Y'know, buys 'er own drinks - daft bugger! If it wasn't for 'er 'e'd be goin' to the Dogs or the bettin' shop. So I say, 'What the hell?' An' it gives me a break. I mean, 'e's a right randy sod."

"So what happened?" Paula asked, fascinated.

"Well, I 'eard this fat cow from Carlton Street was callin' me 'usband and Dora, that's 'is fancy bit. Slaggin' 'em off, she was. Every Friday night in the pub. Makin' 'em feel uncomfortable, wasn't 'arf layin' into Dora. Goin' out with married men, she said. Breakin' up 'omes. Load o' rubbish like that. Y'know, in front of everybody.

"Well, I wasn't 'avin' that. I mean, this old bag, 'er 'usband buggered off an' left 'er years ago. He was a boozer, an alcoholic. I reckon 'e must 'ave sobered up one mornin' an' seen what she looked like." Terry laughed aloud. "Anyhow, I was ready for 'er last Friday. I got the girl next door to watch the kids an' I went down to the pub. She didn't know I was there. Standin' right behind 'er, I was. An' soon as she started I clocked 'er one. I was that mad I'd 'ave flattened Mike Tyson.

"Well, the landlord calls the police, doesn't 'e? So I tells me 'usband 'arry an' 'is Dora to 'op it quick. An' this snotty young copper starts goin' on at me when it was 'er what started it. He said 'e 'ad to caution me. Anythin' I said would be taken down. So I said, 'Knickers.' An' 'e got all stroppy. He said that wasn't funny an' 'e'd 'eard it dozens o' times. So I said, 'How about this then?' An' I poured a pint o' bitter in 'is 'at. Then 'e got really uptight, but it wasn't my fault. I didn't start it. She did. That cow from Carlton Street." She smiled cheerfully at Paula, took a good swig at her Bacardi and coke and smacked her lips. "What 'ave you bin up to then?"

"Nothing really," Paula said, feeling as though she was letting the side down. "I lost my husband. He died just a couple of weeks ago."

"Oh no!" Terry looked genuinely shocked. "I'd 'ate that. I'd 'ate to lose my 'arry."

"Mother!" Paula's elder daughter confronted her accusingly. "You've been drinking."

"Have I, dear?" The taxi driver had helped her from his cab with a knowing, 'Mind 'ow you go now,' and she had suddenly realised how an elderly lady must feel when she is not sure her limbs will support her. 'Legless,' they called it. Very apt, thought Paula. But she was far from legless and well aware of her daughters' disapproval.

"People drink to forget," the younger daughter said, with a hint of compassion.

"I don't want to forget anything," Paula said. "And I certainly don't want to forget your father." She smiled fondly at the framed photograph of her husband on the sideboard. "He was a lovely man and I loved him. I always loved him." She knew she would not have been able to say this if she hadn't had a couple of glasses of sherry. But she was glad she had said it. In all the years they had been married she had never actually told him and she wished he was here now so she could tell him to his face. "So you can stop worrying. The pair of you. I am not going to turn into a maudlin alcoholic. I am not going to turn into a maudlin anything."

"It's that Jim Ponsonby," Alison, the elder daughter, said. "Geoffrey says he's a pseud."

"Who's a pseud, dear?" Paula asked innocently. "Geoffrey?"

"Jim Ponsonby!"

"He's always in the White Lion," the younger girl, Pam, said. "Every lunch time. Eleven 'til three."

"Well, I did see Mr Ponsonby this morning and I have been in the White Lion. But not with Mr Ponsonby."

"You've been in the White Lion?" Both daughters looked at her aghast. "*You*?"

"Yes," Paula replied. "*Me*! And why shouldn't I? All it says outside is: No persons under the age of ..."

"Who were you with?" Alison demanded, as if of a wayward child.

"Perhaps," Paula said, "you would care to re-phrase that question."

"Who were you with, Mum?" Pam asked gently.

"That's better." Paula put the kettle on, purposely making them wait. "I was with a very nice girl, the mother of three young children and the loyal wife of a philandering husband. A lovely girl with a penchant for pouring pints of beer into policemen's hats."

Not for the first time it occurred to Paula that the so-called underprivileged often lead more interesting and eventful lives than the supposedly better off.

"Her name is Terry," she said, with a smile.

The girls looked at each other, convinced their mother was more than slightly tipsy. She wouldn't normally use words like penchant. And who was this Terry, mother of three? It was no one they knew and the elder girl was growing more and more restive. She hadn't been to Sainsbury's yet and there were several things Geoffrey wanted her to put to her mother.

For one thing, there was the house. It was too big for Paula now, on her own. According to Geoffrey, all that capital could be freed and put to better use. And Ted must have left a few bob, Geoffrey said. There were matters to discuss, things to be sorted out and the sooner the better. They could move to a bigger house, for instance, with a granny flat for her mother. But, for the moment, granny wasn't making any sense.

"Mother," Alison said stridently, "you are not making any sense."

"She was," Paula said. "The girl I was with in the White Lion. She was making very good sense. She told me I should take myself off for a good holiday."

"Well yes, of course, Mum," the younger girl agreed at once. "You could have a few days in North Wales or Scarborough. You like Scarborough."

Paula turned away and smiled to herself. North

Wales? Scarborough? As Terry or Rose might say: Sod Scarborough! It was not that kind of holiday she had in mind.

"But what do *you* want to do?" Rose was the first and only one to ask that question.

"I don't know," Paula said. "But I know what I don't want to do. I don't want to sell up and help Geoffrey buy a bigger house with a granny flat. I don't want to live in a granny flat. I may be a granny but I don't feel like one. When I was a girl grannies were old. I'm not old. At least, I don't feel old. And anyway, I've got two daughters, not one. Geoffrey tends to forget Pam when it suits him."

"Geoffrey?" Rose didn't like Paula's son-in-law. She couldn't stand him. The supercilious twit, as she called him, had arrived at the house one day and Rose had answered his knock at the door. Geoffrey had treated her as if she was the cleaning lady. "You take no notice of bloody Geoffrey," she said. "He'll have you sold up and measured for a box if you let him."

"There's no chance of that, Rose," Paula assured her. "I'd rather die than live with Geoffrey."

"And what does Pam think you should do?"

"She hasn't said. But she keeps on about how she hates her job. How she'd like to be free. Financially independent, she calls it. She's suddenly become an expert on Inheritance Tax and how one can 'ease the tax burden' by making regular gifts to one's children and providing one lives for seven years they have no tax to pay."

"Seven years? You're fifty bloody four! You'll live for ages yet. Listen, everything they say and do just proves they're only interested in themselves. You must put yourself first for a change. They don't need you, not any more. They have their whole lives ahead of them."

Paula smiled. "Rose," she said fondly, "you are the only sane, objective person I know."

"I don't know about sane," Rose said.

Paula ignored the interruption. "And that's why I want to consult you, see what you think."

Rose stopped dusting.

"I have a nice house, paid for, and no other debts," Paula began. "I have a good income from investments, so I suppose I'm what Pam calls 'financially independent'. Now my dear husband, Ted, left a little note with his solicitor friend, a Mr Ponsonby, to the effect that there is a separate account at the bank which holds about twenty five thousand pounds.

"The note says, among other things, that I now have the time and the money to do something strictly for myself. He wants me to spend this money in whatever way I wish. But it must be on myself and what I want - nobody else. Clothes, holidays, anything, it doesn't matter what. But it must be on me. 'Do not,' the note says, 'under any circumstances pass the money on to the girls. They'll only spend it. And money,' it says, 'like youth, is wasted on the young.' He wants me to spend it and, in big letters, ENJOY IT!"

Rose clapped her hands. "I always liked your husband. He was nice to everyone, a real gentleman. And he always knew what was what."

"Rose," Paula said soberly, "I want to go away somewhere, somewhere different. I want to do something different, something I've never done before. But I don't want to go on my own."

Chapter Two

They had raided Knightsbridge - Harrods, Harvey Nicols *et al* - and with their newly created hairstyles and expensive-looking shopping bags Paula and Rose returned to the Savoy as bubbly and sparkling as the champagne they had quaffed with their pub lunch. They were ravenous now and ready to eat in the celebrated Grill Room where they soon caught the eye of a well-heeled if overweight, cigar-wielding gentleman who was dining alone. He smiled expansively, waved his cigar and they returned his greeting with cautious nods.

"Who's he?" Rose demanded.

"How should I know?" Paula said, with a laugh. "He's probably a white slave trader plotting to whisk us away to some harem in Marrakesh."

"Ooh!" Rose looked hopeful. "Do you reckon?"

He was there again when they went upstairs to the American Bar and this time he sent the waiter over.

"If you ladies are free," the waiter said, "the gentleman in the corner would very much like you to have a drink with him."

"Tell him we're far from free," Rose said. "We're very expensive."

"Rose!" Paula cautioned as the waiter frowned and moved away. "You'll get us thrown out. They'll think we're prostitutes or something."

"Hookers," Rose said. "They call 'em hookers."

The cigar appeared close to Rose's ear. "I sure hope I didn't offend you ladies," the owner said in a nasal drawl. "I kinda forget when I'm over here. You folks are sorta more reserved ..."

He had a pleasant, open face and a respectful way with him. Paula smiled. "That's all right."

"It's just that our mothers told us never to speak to strange men," Rose told him.

"I ain't strange," the man said, pretending to be hurt. "I'm an American."

"Exactly," Rose said.

They all laughed and the American took this as an invitation to pull out a chair and sit down. He switched his cigar and held out a hand. "Chuck," he said. "Chuck Manners."

"Mrs Paula Blossom," Paula said, "and Mrs Rose Parker."

"Widowed," Rose added. "Both of us."

"Gee," said Chuck. "I'm sorry."

"Is your name really 'Chuck'?" Rose asked.

"Charles - but I guess I got stuck with Chuck in high school."

Rose laughed and Chuck looked mildly surprised.

"It's just that where we come from," she told him, "people call each other 'Chuck' all the time."

"And where would that be?"

"Up North."

"It's a term of endearment," Paula explained.

"That so?" He smiled. "Divided by a common language, huh? We had this young guy come over from Ireland once, name of Paddy McCann. He picks up a cab at Kennedy, the cab driver says, 'Where to, Mac?' And, according to the cab driver, Paddy says, 'Do I know you?' "

He was from Omaha, Nebraska, he told them, but he hadn't been home in years. He lived in California.

He was in the movie business.

Rose's interest quickened. "Hollywood?"

"Well, I try not to spend too much time there."

"What do you do, Mr Manners?" Paula asked.

"I wish you'd call me 'Chuck'," he said, with his wide smile. "I'm a sorta entrepreneur."

"A sorta what?" Rose asked.

"A sorta go-between. I bring people together. People who want to make movies and people who can put up the money. I have one or two people here to see then, if all goes well, I'm off to Cannes for the festival."

"Cannes?" they echoed. "The film festival?"

They looked at each other eagerly.

"The South of France," Paula said.

"The French Riviera," Rose said.

"You know Cannes?" Chuck asked.

They shook their heads.

"But we're lookin' for somewhere to go," Rose said.

"We're off on a little holiday," Paula explained.

Chuck shook his head. "You wouldn't get a hotel room in Cannes right now. Darned near impossible."

"Oh, we'd find somewhere," Rose said confidently.

"No, really," Chuck insisted. "No kiddin'. The place is full of movie people this time of year. Hotels booked up months in advance."

"I suppose so," Paula accepted.

But Rose would not be put off. "No. I want to go to Cannes. We'll get in somewhere. And we might see some film stars. I used to love going to the pictures. All those lovely leading men. Clark Gable, Gary Cooper, Cary Grant ..."

"They're all dead," Paula said.

Chuck was charmed. "You like movie stars, huh?"

"I used to like Richard Burton," Paula said quietly.

"I like the younger ones, too," Rose said. "That Richard Gere - the way he carried Debra Whatsit off out of the factory. I bet he could make your toes curl."

"Let me get you ladies a drink," Chuck said, trying to catch the waiter's eye. But the American Bar had filled up. A group of Japanese tourists looking like a swarm of paparazzi with their ever present cameras had, as usual, cornered a large share of the market and the waiter was deluged with demands for soft drinks.

"Don't go away now," Chuck said and he went to the bar. Paula took the opportunity to go to the ladies room.

Rose looked around at the affluent-looking males in sober business suits, the obvious tourists and here and there a well-dressed female. She held her head high, shook out her tight black curls and lit a fresh cigarette. She could really get used to this life, she told herself. No problem.

"Paula gone to powder her nose?" Chuck asked, with a tray full of drinks and small mixer bottles.

"No," Rose said. "She's gone for a pee."

Chuck let out a deep belly laugh, rattling the drinks on the tray. "You really are somethin', Rosie. You know that?"

Rose plied him with questions about films and the people in them and good-naturedly he answered as best he could.

"We must go to Cannes," she said decisively.

Chuck shook his head. "Cannes is pretty expensive any time but these two weeks things go through the roof. They really do."

"That's no problem," Rose said airily. "We've got

pots of money. We're going on holiday and we can afford to go anywhere in the world."

"That so?" He thought for a moment then he leaned forward earnestly, his voice lowered. "No kiddin' now, Rosie. Are you guys really rich? I mean, *seriously.*"

"Is there any other way?"

"You know what I mean," he said, refusing to be put off. "Are you really loaded?"

"Like a couple of Clint Eastwood's magnums," Rose said, waving him away.

"No, don't get me wrong. I mean, what I want to say is, if you'd like to get into the movie business there really are some big notes to be made and you can have fun along the way."

Rose smiled at him, like a conspirator. "Okay. So we're rich. *Seriously.*"

Paula came back and resumed her seat.

"You've been a long time," Rose commented.

"I saw this brochure on Bali and the Far East," she said. "Looks interesting."

"Nah!" Rose said. "I knew a girl who went to the Far East once. Bangkok, I think it was. Spent most of her time on the bog."

Paula smiled helplessly at Chuck. "I'm afraid Rose doesn't wrap things up."

"So I've noticed," he replied.

"Chuck knows all the big names," Rose rushed on. "Redford, De Niro, Meryl Streep, Dustin thing - he's met them all. And he's convinced me, Paula. Cannes is the place for us. At least, for the next two weeks."

"But where would we stay?"

"Listen, ladies." Chuck had apparently changed his mind. "Let me make a call." Ten minutes later he was back, all smiles. "There's this little guy in Cannes who kinda owes me a favour. If he can't find you a place, no one can. Knows the town like a native."

"Is he French?"

"No, no. He's as English as your Big Ben."

The waiter came, apologising for neglecting them. "Could I get an envelope and some writing paper?" Chuck asked. "Single sheet would be fine."

"Certainly, sir," the waiter said, pleased to be of help.

"I'll give you a letter of intro," Chuck told Paula and Rose. "He'll take good care of you. Herbie's the name. Herbie Kay. Probably get you in at the Carlton."

Back in their room, with the help of the travelling kettle she'd brought along to make sure of a decent cup of tea, Rose steamed open the envelope and handed the note to Paula.

"Dear Herb," Paula read aloud. "These are the two broads I was telling you about. Mrs Paula Blossom and Mrs Rose Parker. I reckon they really are loaded, a couple of seriously rich widows. Could be they are just the little angels you've been looking for. If I'm right, they're all yours. If I'm not then, like I said, you can play them off against the sheik. Will ring Friday, yours Chuck. PS: Go easy on them, Herb. They may be dumb but I reckon they're nice people."

Rose exploded. "Dumb, are we?"

"Why do you suppose he thinks we're rich?" Paula asked, eyeing Rose with some suspicion.

Rose struck an elegant pose. "It's the clothes, the hair-do's. We got class now, kid. We look like a million dollars - each!" She thought for a moment. "I suppose I should start talking posh."

"I think our Mr Manners is hoping to use us to play

some kind of practical joke on his friend Herb - whoever Herb might be."

"He called us angels," Rose reminded her with a flourish.

Paula nodded. "I believe that's what theatrical producers call people who put up the money for their shows."

"He's in the film business."

"Same thing. Film producers need backers."

"So that's his hard luck. If he thinks we're loaded then let him. He calls us 'broads' and he says we're dumb. If he wants to find a room in Cannes for a couple of dumb broads that's fine by me."

The arrivals hall at Nice airport was crowded. Taxi drivers and couriers, holding up signboards, milled at the foot of the stairway.

"There!" Rose shrieked. "What does that say?"

"Where?" Paula a little short-sighted, screwed up her eyes to scan the boards and upturned faces.

A taxi driver approached, holding up a small blackboard with the word 'Bosom' written in chalk. "*Madame* Bosom?"

"Must mean you," Rose said. "I've got a chest like a sand dancer's stand-in."

Dolefully, the long gaunt taxi driver shook his head. "*Non*? Is not you?"

"Blossom," Paula said. "Mrs Blossom."

"Ah! Mrs Bosom!" His craggy face broke into a huge smile and he hand-wrestled briefly with the porter who had claimed their cases. Unfamiliar curses ensued. Then Paula paid off the porter with a flurry of apologies and they hurried after the driver who was swiftly departing with their luggage.

"Where are we going?" Rose demanded as the taxi, to an angry chorus of motor horns, was thrust out on to the Promenade des Anglais.

The taxi driver threw insults from his open window, gesticulating at other motorists with his free hand. Then, mildly and courteously, over his shoulder, he informed his captive passengers, "To the Carlton. *M'sieur* Kay say to bring you to the Carlton."

"Better be good - this Carlton," Rose warned him.

"*Le Carlton, madame*?" The driver seemed genuinely shocked. "*Le Carlton, c'est magnifique*! The best, the most famous hotel *à Cannes*."

The lobby with its wide grey carpet was like a stage set. Sometimes it was the floor of a hall of commerce, sometimes the apron of some glossy reception. Today, and for most of the next two weeks, it resembled the street scene at the opening of *Guys and Dolls*.

Men stood around in small groups chatting noisily or in pairs conferring quietly and intently. Old friends greeted each other as if at a school reunion and none were more raucous than an all-women huddle over by the desk. Hopeful girls hovered as the more mature, more elegantly dressed stood aloof or sat upright on the comfortable sofas. Older players, their reputations secure, appeared more relaxed, more casually dressed, confident in their membership of the club.

Press and publicity people mingled. Pushy and persistent female journalists, their jaws set, did their best to outdo their male counterparts. Photographers, all of them male, argued and remonstrated with an under manager who had ruled that photography was not permitted in the hotel foyer. And Paula and Rose were caught up at once in the sheer excitement of the place as the driver delivered them to the desk and a lobby boy relieved him of their luggage.

"We should have bought some new cases," Paula said.

"No, no," Rose said in her new, posh voice. "My suitcase was good enough for Benidorm and it's good enough for here. Shows you don't care."

The young man behind the high, polished reception desk smiled at her.

"Isn't that right, cock?" she asked.

The smile didn't falter. "*Oui, madame*. Anything you say."

He watched as they signed in, then he turned to Paula. "I have a message for you, madam," he told her in beautifully modulated English. "From a gentleman. A Mr Kay."

It was a note on a small white card. 'Ladies, I await your arrival with pleasure. When you have settled in, please have me paged at the desk. Yours, Herbert H. Kay.'

Two of the lobby boys led them to the lift and up to their room. It was a large, white, high-ceilinged room overlooking the Croisette, the palm trees along the seafront and the blue grey Mediterranean beyond. Rose threw open the balcony windows. "Wow!" she exclaimed. "What a view!"

"Mr Herbert H. Kay has done us proud," Paula said, taking in the furnishings: the white wicker table and two chairs, the twin beds, the long dressing table, the little writing desk and, by the window, the cheval-glass swing mirror. "I think we'd better put him right,

Rose."

Rose was out on the balcony, waving enthusiastically at a couple of tanned beach boys. "About what?"

"About us. He obviously thinks we're millionaires or something. Probably wants us to finance his next epic."

"Well, that's all right. He can think what he likes. We'll just go along with it, that's all. Live now for tomorrow - who knows?"

"We can't do that. I'll tell him this evening. We're just here for a holiday." Paula laughed. "I should think this place'll take most of our money, anyway."

Rose had kicked off her shoes. Now she found one and hobbled about the room in search of the other. "Tell you what," she said, as she searched, "you start to unpack and I'll go down and find out what the room rate is. See how we stand."

She found the missing shoe and went down to the lobby. It was a different man on the desk.

"Can I have the room rates, please?"

"*Madame*?"

"A list of charges. For the room."

"We have no rooms at present, *madame*. Every room in the hotel is taken for this week and for the next."

"I don't want a room. I've got a room. I just want to know what the hell it's going to cost."

The man looked perplexed. He peered around behind the desk as if he knew he was not going to find what the lady wanted. Then he went behind the scenes and came back with a duplicated, coffee-stained sheet. "Is all we have," he said, he shoulders hunched apologetically. "You may take it if you wish."

It occurred to Rose that this must be the kind of place where if you need to ask how much you probably can't afford it. "Oh right. Thanks." she said, taking the dingy-looking sheet. "And will you page Mr Herbert H. Kay for me, please?"

The man behind the desk, who had suddenly seemed distracted, came back with a jolt. "Mr Herbert H.Kay? Certainly, *madame*. At once. *Tout de suite*!" He called over a small boy in a pillbox hat and a high-buttoned uniform that, like many aspects of this hotel, seemed to belong to a past era. Then he turned back to Rose, perplexed yet again. "But that is *M'sieur* Kay, *madame*. Over there."

"So it is," Rose said with a smile. To the boy she said, "Get him for me, sonny. Mr Kay. Tell him Mrs Rose Parker wants a word."

Quietly, in brisk French, the man behind the desk passed on her instructions and the page boy hurried over to Mr Herbert H.Kay's side.

The man he approached was a short, thick-set man with a near bald head and bushy black eyebrows. He looked across at Rose, excused himself and came to greet her. "Mrs Parker," he said, with a flourish of his unlit cigar. "How very nice to meet you."

The polished veneer of his voice was transparent - at least to Rose. "Was it Catford or Stepney?"

For a brief instant the worldly-wise Herbert H.Kay was thrown. "How's that?"

"My late husband was a Cockney, Mr Kay. I'd spot those velvet tones anywhere."

He laughed. "You and I are going to have fun, Mrs Parker."

"In that case," she said, "You'd better call me Rose."

He kissed her hand. "Herbie. Herbie Kay."

"Could we sit down for a moment?"
"Sure. Do you want a drink? Coffee or something?"
"No. I just came down to have a quick word."
"Everything's all right, I hope? Your room ..."
"Is fine. No, it's about my friend Mrs Blossom."
"What is it? She okay?"
"Oh, yes. She's fine. Her name's Paula, by the way. But I'll introduce you later. The thing is with Paula, it's money."
"Money?"
"Money." Rose looked him in the eye. "The thing is, she's got so much of it she just doesn't know what to do with it all."
"Is that so?"
"You see, my old man - my husband, that is - he left me pretty well placed. Money is just no problem any more. But Paula - wow! She's got more noughts to her name than the National Lottery."
A little embarrassed, Herbie feigned incuriosity as if more than a little puzzled as to how Paula's wealth or lack of it could possibly concern him.
"Now the reason I'm telling you this," Rose went on, "is because she likes to pretend she's a lady of ... well ... limited means."
"Very wise," Herbie said, nodding soberly.
"But take no notice, Herbie. The lady is loaded. And we're here to have a good time. We'd like to start by meeting some of your film star friends."
He was smiling now, flourishing his cigar again.
"But you mustn't tell her I told you this," Rose insisted. "You do understand, don't you?"
"Sure," he said. "Sure I understand. And you can rely on me, Rosie. You ladies are gonna have the time of your lives."

Chapter Three

The bar was crowded. Elegantly dressed and coiffed women, young and old, along with smartly turned out, mainly older men, many in dinner jacket and black tie, were being jostled and crushed in the heaving maelstrom of the L-shaped room. As if by right and looking slightly disreputable in his red bow tie, Herbie Kay was installed at one end of the long bar. Paula and Rose, clutching their evening bags, aware of the display of expensive jewellery and the paucity of their own, hovered in the entrance.

"Really," Rose said loudly and in her new posh voice, "I don't see the point in owning such fabulous rocks if they're too valuable to be worn in public."

"We'll have to have replicas made," Paula said, taking the cue with a laugh. "If only for safety's sake."

"Well, of course," Rose went on. "I mean, one can't tell if they're worth a fortune or a packet of fags when they're on." She stared pointedly at a glittering necklace at a nearby wrinkled throat. "Can you, cock?"

The woman addressed looked down her nose at Rose and turned away as Herbie Kay, cutting a swath through the crowd like a speedboat on a yachting lake, swept towards them.

"Ladies! Lovely ladies!" he gushed. "How nice to see you. You light up my night."

"Your evening, Herb," Rose corrected. "We have to be in bed when the clock strikes twelve."

"Well, that can be arranged," he said with a grin. "Now this must be the lovely Paula - Mrs Blossom."

Paula glanced at Rose who explained feebly that

she had met Herbie when she came down to the desk. "Didn't I tell you?"

"No, Rose, you didn't," Paula said. "I'm very pleased to meet you, Mr Kay, and I must thank you for finding such a lovely room for us."

"You like it?"

"It's lovely. Especially now, after dark, with all those lights strung out along the seafront."

Herbie seemed genuinely pleased. "Come on," he said. "Let me introduce you to some of my friends."

Paula and Rose hurried along the narrow path through the crowd that seemed to open before him as if he was Moses parting the Red Sea.

"Allow me to introduce these lovely ladies from England," he began.

"Phew!" Rose breathed thankfully. "It's like a rugby scrum back there."

A tall, haughty-looking woman in her sixties flicked the ash from her cigarette in its long holder and said coolly, "I've never been in a rugby scrum."

Rose looked her up and down. "You'd love it, cock. You bend down and some big, hairy rugby player shoves his head up your backside."

"Yeah, well, er..." Even Herbie was non-plussed.

The others in Herbie's circle reacted with muted amusement, all except a doddering old man who Paula guessed was the woman's husband. He glared at Rose with undisguised hostility as his wife threw back her head and gazed out above the crowd as if to imply she was above this intrusive rabble.

An obviously sophisticated lady, whose face Paula found vaguely familiar, turned away to hide her smile. Her escort, a corpulent man whose large, heavy body was supported by very short, thick legs, and whose mane of white hair framed his leonine features merely drew on his cigar, puffed out smoke and grinned as if to say he'd seen and heard it all before.

A strikingly pretty girl and her darkly handsome partner maintained their fixed smiles, unaware of any tension. She was Italian and he was French and their grasp of English was not strong.

The other member of Herbie's party was a tallish, worldly-looking man in his mid-fifties. He still had his own dark hair, flecked with grey now, and most of his own teeth, and he was good-looking in a quiet, distinguished way. Paula noticed he was not smoking and guessed from his nicotine-free fingers he was not a smoker - a bonus point in Paula's book. She also noticed how he returned her smile with an unexpected warmth and a perceptible quickening of interest.

"Jim and his dear wife Edna," Herbie said, introducing the dinosauric old man and his elongated wife.

"Edina," the wife corrected.

Herbie smiled and nodded. "Jim and Edna."

The old man was still glaring but both Paula and Rose had realised this was his normal expression. He appeared to be almost totally deaf and though he knew when something was being said he was obviously not sure what. It was this, perhaps, that caused him to glare. It didn't matter here because people knew who he was and what he had been. Most were respectful, even reverential.

"You must have seen his pictures," Herbie said. "He was a master of suspense - old Jim."

Rose opened her mouth but a glance from Paula

forbade her to comment.

Herbie then introduced the sophisticated lady and Paula and Rose took to her at once. She had a smiling, open manner and a total lack of pretension.

"Laura," Herbie said. "Laura ..."

At once Rose cut in. "It's not! You're not!"

"Laura Baker," Paula said in disbelief. "I used to love your films. I thought you were lovely when ..."

"When I was young?" Laura said, with a laugh.

Paula looked embarrassed and Rose attempted to come to the rescue. "Don't worry about it," she told Laura, who clearly wasn't worried. "As we say back home, better to be a has been than a never was."

"Well, thank you very much," Laura said, pretending to be miffed. "And I thought I was going to like you."

They were joined now by another beauty a little younger than Laura. Herbie Kay greeted her with a kiss on the cheek. "Arlene, sweetheart, late as always."

Arlene seemed to know everyone except Paula and Rose. She smiled carelessly and easily as if to say she had been late for far bigger do's than this. Again, as there had been with Laura, there was something vaguely familiar about her.

With her green eyes and thick copper coloured hair she was still, despite the years, a beautiful woman, and all this middle-aged pulchritude, not to mention the quite gorgeous Italian *ingénue* by her side, was making Paula feel inadequate. Not so Rose.

Herbie introduced Arlene and Rose said, "I know the face but I can't place it."

"That lovely face," Herbie said expansively, "has made a lot of movies."

"Mm," Rose murmured, still puzzling. "But we don't

go to the pictures much, do we, Paula?"

Herbie pretended to be horrified. "Don't go to the pictures? You can't make statements like that! This is Cannes!"

"We see lots of pictures on the television," Paula offered. "I thought you were lovely in that one in Rome."

Arlene nodded and smiled. "I enjoyed making that."

"One of the few of Arlene's movies I had nothing to do with," the short, white-haired man at Laura's side said.

A realisation dawned on Rose. "Is that the one where you had to swim with nowt on?"

Paula couldn't remember the title of the film but one scene had stuck in her memory and probably in the memories of thousands of others. Arlene had played the part of a mysterious contessa who walked sedately every morning from her hillside villa to her swimming pool where she removed her dressing gown, climbed the steps to the diving board and stood for several breathtaking seconds, statuesque and completely naked, before diving in.

"Rose!" Paula said. "Don't you mean 'in the nude'?"

Rose laughed. "That's what I said. 'With nowt on'."

"That's the one," Arlene confirmed.

"What's it like?" Rose asked. "I mean, with all those people and cameras and things."

Arlene shrugged. "You don't think about it. You just do it. It's only a movie."

"I don't think I could do it," Rose said.

"I certainly couldn't," Laura cut in, "and I never have. But only because I don't have the figure for it."

"What about you, Paula?" Rose asked.

"Well," Paula said. "I wouldn't mind - if I had a

body like Arlene's."

"Right," Rose agreed. "If you've got it, flaunt it."

"I wouldn't say that Arlene flaunted it exactly," the white-haired man protested. "In the movie it was part of the story. If it's part of the story it's okay."

"What a load o' rubbish," Rose laughed. "They stick those scenes in whenever it gets boring. I can just see the director. This parts a bit dead, he thinks. So it's come on, girls, get 'em off!"

The man looked around for support but neither Laura nor Arlene came to his aid.

"I'm with Rose on this one," Laura told him. "I can remember you trying to get me to take my clothes off."

"Ah!" the man said, with a mischievous grin. "But that wasn't in a movie."

They all laughed and Herbie Kay said, "Girls take off their clothes at the drop of a hat these days."

And they all laughed again, this time at Herbie's surprisingly pompous pronouncement. But the giraffe-like Edina suddenly re-entered the conversation. "You should see them on the beach," she said furiously. "They lie there with their bare breasts sticking up. Jim says they're like soldiers on parade, waiting for inspection."

Her husband glared and Laura said, "It's a bit chilly for that, Edina. There's quite a breeze out there."

"I'll say there is," Rose added. "I reckon even my boobs would stand to attention."

With so many interruptions Herbie had not quite completed the formalities. The quiet man turned from the bar to distribute drinks. When everyone had one he smiled at Paula. "My name's Tom, by the way."

"Paula," she said. "Paula Blossom."

"Blossom - now that's an unusual name," he said.

"I'm sure there's a joke or two in there, but I expect you've heard them all."

"Tom Daniels," Herbie butted in with a belated introduction. "I'm a great fan of his brother Jack."

She looked puzzled for a moment then Tom said, "He means the whisky. He says it every time."

Paula felt her responses had atrophied somewhat in suburbia. Now she was revelling in the racy, inconsequential exchanges. "And where do you fit into all this, Mr Daniels?"

"Tom - please," he said.

"He's a screen-writer," Herbie told her. "The best."

"A writer?"

"A screen-writer," Tom said. "I never got round to writing a book." He smiled ruefully. "Which is something I always planned to do and never did."

"There's still time," Paula said. "Surely?"

"I have to earn my living, Mrs Blossom."

"Paula - please."

Herbie could see they didn't need him. They were getting on fine. He turned back to the others.

"Don't you like screen-writing?" Paula asked.

"Oh, sure," he said. "It's my job. It's what I do and, fortunately, it keeps me in the manner to which I'm afraid I've become accustomed."

"But you'd rather write books?"

"Well, yes," he admitted, a little surprised that he was saying this to someone he had only just met.

"Couldn't you take a year off or something?"

"I could. But when I got back I'd find the circus had left town. You have to stay with this business on the inside. Otherwise you find yourself locked out."

Paula liked his voice and she wanted him to go on

talking. "What are you working on now?"

"Nothing specific," he said. "But I guess something will come out of this week or next. An original, maybe."

"An original screenplay? Sounds awfully difficult. I mean, how do you find your stories?"

He laughed. "If it's a story you want you only have to look around. I guess we could start right here with a story about two mysterious ladies who come out from England and go straight to the heart of the world's most famous film festival."

"We're not mysterious. We're just here on holiday."

Tom looked her in the eyes and she found she liked him even more. He had a quiet confidence about him and there was something in his relaxed manner that reminded her of her husband Ted.

"Two mysterious ladies," he insisted.

"Come on, you two," Herbie said, with Rose on his arm. "We're going to eat."

They went to a restaurant on the old port. There were ten of them for dinner and the place was crowded but, as usual, Herbie had made the necessary arrangements. A large round table in a comfortable corner awaited them.

"*M'sieur* Kay," the fat lady *patronne* complained. "You are late."

With a smile of resignation her husband handed out the ridiculously large menus. "*M'sieur* Kay is always late."

The actress, Arlene, whom Herbie had good-naturedly rebuked for being late, smiled at him in sweet revenge and he held up his hands. "Hoist with me own whatsit!" He turned to the fat lady *patronne*. "But worth waiting for, eh *maman*?" He kissed her on the cheek and she responded with a fluttering, "*Ooh la la*!"

Paula found herself flanked by contrasts. On her right was the darkly handsome French actor, on her left the geriatric Jim. Her new-found screen-writer friend had been too polite to shoulder his way in beside her. Or perhaps, she thought, he hadn't wanted to.

The young actor really was handsome. Thick black curls lay in abundance on his white collar and, Paula noticed, he had the kind of long black eyelashes some women would kill for.

"Phillipe," she said softly. "Is there something wrong? You seem so sad."

"I am so sad," he agreed mournfully.

"Would you like to talk about it? You know what they say - a problem shared"

"*Comment*?"

No, she thought, perhaps you don't. He was watching, brooding over the way a man old enough to be her father was ogling the Italian girl.

Paula turned to Jim whose grizzled head was down almost in his soup. "Who is that man over there, Jim?"

"What man? Where?"

"Sitting next to Miss Carr." Paula had recognised the film actress Dierdre Carr. She was in her late fifties now and she had something of the serene look of the late Princess Grace of Monaco. The man next to her was as ugly as she was beautiful. He was thick-set, bald and heavy jowled, and he put Paula in mind of a boar's head on a festive table. He was spooning his soup with slow, calculated movements as if feeding a baby and he was making as much mess.

"He's a shit!" Jim announced loudly and he glared

across the room.

Rose, who was facing Paula and Jim across the table on Herbie's left, looked over her shoulder at the man in question. "And does he have a name - this shit?"

Herbie looked worried. "He's a producer - and a big one, too. Very influential. An important man. Marvyn Brodsky. Pulled in some pretty big grosses in his time."

"A shit!" insisted Jim, who was supposed to be deaf.

"Got the hots for Nina," Herbie said quietly.

"Phillipe's girl?" Rose was affronted. "Why he's old enough to be her grandfather. And he's an ugly bugger, too. Talk about Beauty and the Beast!"

Phillipe looked up, his dark eyes narrowed with hate. "I kill heem. He spick with Nina, I kill heem."

Nina, who was seated between Tom the screen-writer and Laura Baker, suddenly erupted. "I spick with heem. You keep off my bees-ness. Marvyn geeve me part in new movie. I go to 'ollywood."

Marvyn Brodsky was coming over, as if aware that he was under discussion. Herbie Kay stood up to receive him. Herbie introduced Paula and Rose as two of his friends out from England but Brodsky was clearly not interested in them. Rose dismissed him with a curt nod, equally rude, and Paula noticed he had bread-crumbs on one of his several chins and a recent soup stain, brown at the edges, on the lapel of his jacket.

Brodsky evidently knew everyone else. He acknowledged the others and nodded at Jim who pointedly ignored him. He then infuriated Phillipe by singling out Nina for his unwarranted attention. "Ain't this the most gorgeous gal you ever did see? Loren and Lollabrigida rolled into one, the flower of Italy."

Nina preened herself under his appreciative, heavy-lidded gaze and Phillipe stood up angrily, his chair scraping back on the polished tile floor. For a moment he looked dangerous, then he threw down his napkin and stormed out of the restaurant. Paula half-expected Nina to run after him but she didn't.

"I say the wrong thing?" Brodsky asked innocently.

Nina was still preening and playing up to him.

"Phillipe is a bit touchy," Herbie offered.

Paula rarely took an instant dislike to anyone but Marvyn Brodsky proved an exception. Quietly, across the table, she said to Rose, "I think he's far too old to go chasing after girls of Nina's age."

Rose agreed loudly. "He's too old for girls of any age."

"What? What's that?" Brodsky turned to look at Rose but Herbie averted the looming confrontation by steering him away, talking quietly and confidentially to him and returning him to his table.

"Herbie the diplomat," Tom said, with a smile. "If you care about the movies you ladies will have to be a bit more circumspect."

"Circum-what?" Rose said.

"He means that sometimes you got to kiss ass," Arlene said. "Even with a guy like Brodsky."

"I'd rather kiss King Kong's arse than 'is," Rose declared, again forgetting her new posh accent.

"The fact is," Paula said, "we don't care about Brodsky. Or the movies. We're just here to enjoy Cannes."

"I care," Nina said, near to tears. "Meester Brodsky geeve me part in peecture, I 'ope. Now - I don't know what."

"Don't worry," Paula said, with totally unfounded

confidence. "We'll help you get into pictures."

"Sure we will." Rose flourished an imaginary cigar. Then she realised Paula had inadvertently implied that they were women of influence. She turned to Arlene and Laura Baker. "Do people get offered parts here?"

"Not often, Rose," Arlene said. "There's always a lot of talk. Big talk, empty talk. Most people come here to see and be seen. The 'phone calls come later, if at all."

"There are always those on the fringe trying to push some project or other," Laura added. "You had a script this morning."

Arlene laughed. "Oh that," she said. "The synopsis was enough to put me off."

"What was it about?" Rose asked eagerly.

"It's supposed to be the ultimate in sci-fi. Or so it says on the cover. It's about a guy who gets struck by a meteorite or something like that and he develops an enormous penis and an uncontrollable sex drive."

"What was your part?" Rose asked, almost convulsed.

"They wanted me to play his wife," Arlene said and all except Nina and Jim dissolved into fits of laughter.

"In the end," Arlene went on, "the only way I can survive is by cutting him down to size with a chain-saw."

"A peecture is a peecture,' Nina said.

"The man's a shit!" Jim said irrelevantly.

Then Herbie came back. "After we've eaten we're off to Monte. Marvyn wants us to join him at the tables."

Nina brightened, preening herself in anticipation.

The taxi took Herbie and Rose and Paula and Tom

from the old port along the coast road to Nice and on to Monaco. Jim and Edina had bid them a glaring goodnight and along with Arlene and Laura had walked back to the Carlton. Phillipe had not returned to the restaurant and Nina had somehow been spirited away in a separate cab by Marvyn Brodsky who said he would see them there. To Paula the party suddenly seemed less than wholesome, as if they were in some way colluding with Brodsky. She would rather have gone back to the hotel.

The atmosphere in the casino did little to raise her spirits. Nobody laughed. Nobody looked happy. The faces at the tables were either tense or devoid of expression. A powdered, pink-haired Barbara Cartland look-alike made mathematical calculations in a little notebook each time she placed a bet. A large, flabby American gentleman sweated profusely and mopped his red, perspiring brow with a large white handkerchief as he moved his diminishing chips on to a succession of losing squares.

"I don't like it here," Paula said.

"Me neither," Tom agreed.

"Then why did we come?"

"Herbie," Tom said. "Sometimes he wins quite a lot of money. He likes to watch the tables and if he feels lucky he joins in."

Rose was urging Herbie to play but Herbie was simply moving around slowly, watching the tables, refusing to be rushed. Marvyn Brodsky was already seated with Nina, who was all big eyes and bulging bosoms, by his side. Paula and Tom drifted out into the foyer.

Neither had much interest in the tables, Paula

because some puritanical streak in her background disapproved of gambling, Tom because he believed he worked too hard for his money to throw it away across some green baize.

The men on the doors to the inner sanctums, Tom said, reminded him of Mafia hit-men. Paula said they reminded her of undertakers. He laughed. "Similar rackets," he said. "I guess they're both in the disposal business."

Outside on the steps they admired the stringed pearls of lights that lit the square and the waterfront and the quays where millions of pounds' worth of private yachts and cabin cruisers were moored on the shimmering water. Soft music came from a discreetly lit, dark green restaurant where a row of black cabs waited.

She looked up at him. "You're not a gambler. You're not a heavy drinker. You must have some vices."

"Blondes," he said. "I like slim, attractive blondes."

Paula laughed. "I used to be one of those."

"Still are, Mrs Blossom." He smiled. "You still are."

Withdrawing slightly, instinctively, Paula looked across to the taxi rank. Two of the drivers were lounging by the first cab. She glanced at her watch.

"Back to Cannes?" Tom suggested quietly.

She nodded. "I think so."

In the cab they were silent, gazing out from their own private darkness at the swaying fronds of the palm trees along the promenades and the wide stretch of moonlit Mediterranean beyond. Tom had made the first move, an opening gambit, and she was not sure how she should respond. She liked him enormously, but she didn't want to get involved. Or rather, she was scared of getting involved.

Paula made her way into the hotel as Tom paid off the driver and followed her inside.

"Would you like a drink? A night cap?"

She hesitated. "I ... I don't think so, Tom. Thank you so much for seeing me home."

Feeling a little foolish, as if she had implied that her father was waiting up for her and she really ought to be in by now, she turned to go.

"See you tomorrow then," Tom said.

"I hope so," she said and as she walked away towards the lifts she was in two minds. She wanted to stay but the old inbred reticence told her she shouldn't. She felt it wouldn't be just a late night drink. There would be more to it than that and she didn't want to commit herself. She was not ready for any new commitment, she decided, and she was not sure she ever would be. Then she laughed at herself. He'd only asked her to have a drink, for goodness sake!

Tom watched her go. She was a good-looking woman, he thought. Shapely, feminine - and she was refined, too. So much more refined than her friend Rose. Not that he disapproved of Rose. Rose was a tonic, a breath of fresh air in the claustrophobic whirl of rumour and conjecture, of half truths and false smiles and even more false promises that suffused these two weeks in Cannes.

Rose was a rough diamond, Tom concluded, whereas Paula had been exquisitely cut and polished. They made an odd pair and he couldn't help wondering what had brought them together.

He frowned. He felt genuinely drawn to Paula but he was aware of a credibility gap. She was said to be rich. According to Herbie, a mega-rich widow. Tom was not interested in her money. He was well able to take care of himself financially and he certainly wasn't looking for a rich widow. But if he pursued Paula it might look that way.

"Hey, Tom!" An actor friend slapped him on the back. "Let me introduce you to these lovely ladies."

The actor, who had fluffed his chance of the really big time about twenty five years earlier and was now as old as Tom if not older, was with two girls of no more than twenty years of age, yet two more hopefuls on the fringe of filmdom. One of the girls held out her hand, palm downwards, as if she wanted Tom to kiss it.

Always the gentleman, Tom took the extended hand and brushed it with his lips, noticing as he bent his head that she was wearing what looked like a chemise as if she'd been only half dressed when the fire alarm went off. She was also without a bra.

The girl giggled appreciatively and as he raised his head he caught a glimpse of Paula. She was facing him across the foyer as the lift doors closed and hid her from view.

Paula awoke to the sound of two vehicles honking angrily out on the Croisette. Lying in the deeply comfortable bed she gazed up at the high pastel blue ceiling. There was something splendidly distinguished about this hotel. Kings and queens or, at least, princes and princesses had stayed here. Certainly the famous from many fields and some, no doubt, who were infamous had passed through its imposing portals. She laughed aloud and told herself: You are turning into an impressionable snob, Paula Blossom.

She remembered Rose, sat up and looked across

at the twin bed. Her laugh had not roused the slim figure that was curled like a question mark in the tangled sheets. There was a light knock at the door. Paula pulled on her dressing gown and slid into her slippers. All smiles and courteous *bonhomie*, a waiter trundled in a breakfast trolley and hovered until she found her purse.

There was a flower, a single red rose lying across a folded napkin, and there was a note attached. 'To Mrs Blossom, the loveliest lady in the whole of Cannes,' Paula read in surprise and amusement. She went to the door to ask who had sent the note but the waiter had gone.

It didn't seem like something Tom would do and, anyway, the last time she saw him he appeared to be otherwise engaged. But who else could it be? Rose stirred in the bed and not quite knowing why Paula stuffed the note in her pocket, out of sight.

"Aspirins," Rose begged from under the bedclothes.

"Have a cup of coffee," Paula suggested.

"Tea! I ordered tea!"

Paula examined the pot. "It is tea. Come on now. Have a cup of tea and a couple of aspirins."

"Herbie wanted me to go horse-riding with him this morning. Me! Horse-riding!"

"You'd probably enjoy it."

"You what? I've got the bloody Grand National goin' on inside me 'ead as it is. I don't need no horse-riding."

"What time did you get in?"

"About three, I think. Herbie was messing about in the casino for ages. I said, 'Are going to play or not?' And he decided no, he wouldn't. But that Brodsky fella was playing, losing a fortune, too, by the look of it. An' all to impress Miss Wannabee."

Paula smiled. Rose's rambling was a mixture of her old spontaneity, her new posh voice and words and phrases she had picked up from Herbie. "Miss Who?"

"Miss Wannabee. That's what Herbie calls young Nina. She wannabee a big movie star."

"Then what did you do?"

"Then we came back here and had a drink in the bar - several drinks actually. I met an old film star. I'm sure you'd have recognised him. And it was such a shame. He still had the face but it had sort of slipped sideways, as though he'd had a face-lift and they'd dropped it - you know what I mean? And him in all those pictures. I used to like him and, you know, it was so embarrassing, I couldn't remember his second name. I knew he was called Robert something."

"Robert Preston?" Paula guessed. "Robert Shaw?"

"No, he was still alive - I think." She laughed. "He was a bit younger than them, but not much. And I felt as if I knew him. I said, 'I used to like you.' And he laughed and said, 'So what did I do wrong?' Nice fella."

"Sounds like you had a good time."

"Yeah, we did," Rose confirmed. "Oh, and we saw that Tom. Thought you might still have been with him. I mean, I think he fancies you."

Chapter Four

Paula went out on to the balcony. It was a bright sunny morning and quite warm with just a few herring-bone stretches of cirrus cloud in the pale blue sky. Already the sandy beach had been raked, the loungers laid out, the umbrellas unfurled, ready for the sun worshippers. She left Rose in bed and went down to the terrace.

She had pulled on a short navy blue blazer over her blue polka-dot dress with a view to taking a walk along the Croisette. But as she came down the steps she saw Tom making his way through the tables and chairs.

"Paula!" He was clearly pleased to see her. "I could say what a great coincidence, what a superb chance encounter, but the truth is I've been sitting out here for nearly an hour, stumbling through *Nice Matin* with the old schoolboy French and keeping one eye on the look-out for you."

"Only one eye?"

He smiled. "Now you may have something planned, of course, but if not I'd like to take you for a drive inland and maybe for lunch somewhere. Some lovely country back there."

"I don't know."

"I need someone sane to talk to, Paula. Everyone's crazy here." A smiling waiter waltzed by with a pyramid of glasses balanced on a tray. "Even the waiters."

"All right," Paula said, surprising herself. "But if we're to be away all morning I must tell Rose. And I must have my specs." She searched in her bag and pulled out the essential spectacles. "Can't read a thing without them."

"You can ring Rose. There's a phone at the desk."

"Four-o-four," a male voice answered.

"Hello?"

"Paula? It's me, Herbie. Hold on."

"Hello, Paula? Where are you?"

"At the desk. Listen, I'm going out for a run with Tom."

"A run? Are you kidding?"

"In the car. A drive. We may stay out for lunch."

"Oh, great!" Rose said. "See you later then. And what did you say? What am I doing with a strange man in our bedroom?" Paula heard her say over her shoulder, "Paula wants to know what I'm doing with a strange man in our bedroom. Are you a strange man?"

"Tell her I must be," she heard Herbie say. "I'm trying to get you to put some clothes on."

"He says I have to get dressed," Rose said into the 'phone. "Have a good time, Paula. See you later."

Tom's car was parked in a street behind the hotel, well away from the Rolls Royces and Ferraris and other gleaming show-pieces in the precious parking spaces out front. It was a rented Renault and not even the latest model. Not that Paula noticed. Most of her married life she had driven small cars, Minis, Polos, Golfs, the usual 'second' car. Her husband had driven a more prestigious vehicle provided by his company. But none of this mattered to Paula. As far as Paula was concerned a car was a car, a means of transport.

They drove out above Cannes and picked up the road to St-Paul-de-Vence, parking on the edge of the small town and walking in along the narrow, cobblestone streets. Paula was enchanted. It was a lovely place and Tom evidently knew it well.

"I stayed here once - years ago - for a whole summer. I was trying to write a novel and chasing this American girl who was working at the Amex office."

"Did you catch her?" Paula asked.

"I'm afraid not," he admitted.

Paula smiled. "So this is a nostalgia trip? We're sort of retracing your steps, are we?"

He nodded. "I was in love with the place."

Paula had the feeling he wanted to tell her more about himself and no doubt in time he would. But for now he wanted her to enjoy St-Paul-de-Vence.

"In those days," he said, surveying the tourists who thronged the square and stepped in and out of gift shops and tiny boutiques, "there was none of this. It's just so crowded now - and I was hoping we might have lunch at the Colombe d'Or."

La Colombe d'Or, he explained, was one of the best known restaurants in the whole of France. More often than not - at this time of year, anyway - considerable influence had to be wielded to secure a reservation, even for a small table for two.

But they were in luck. Tom dropped the name of the glaring ex-producer, Jim, the *maitre d'* promised a table would be available *à deux heures* and old Jim went up several notches in Paula's estimation.

They found a small bar where they could sit under a parasol and watch the passing parade. Paula was not used to alcohol, especially so early in the day, but she agreed to a Cinzano and lemonade to accompany Tom's beer. Then with time to spare they went for a stroll, like the tourists Tom disdained, through the narrow streets.

There was little conversation, just a feeling of togetherness, a closeness she had not felt since her husband died. She liked Tom though she knew little about him and, liking him, she felt guilty, conscious of betraying the man she had loved and lived with for almost thirty three years.

Back at the Colombe d'Or they waited at the bar until their table was ready. This place, Tom told her, really is world famous. You ought to be impressed. But Paula merely laughed and admitted she had never heard of it.

In this room, he went on, Yves Montand and Simone Signoret held their wedding reception. The owner of the restaurant, Monsieur Roux, was one of the witnesses at the marriage ceremony. Picasso and the painter Braque would often sit out on the terrace under the fig tree with Monsieur Roux.

"I used to like Simone Signoret," Paula said. "She certainly had something."

"Yes," Tom agreed. "And yet she was ... comfortable."

"Comfortable?"

"Yes. She had great sex appeal and yet she looked as though she would be relaxed and sort of comfortable to be with. Like you." He smiled. "You are comfortable."

Paula laughed. "Simone Signoret without the sex appeal."

"No, no," Tom said, as a young waitress led them to their table. "I didn't say that."

"To drink, *m'sieur*?"

Tom looked at Paula.

"Perrier."

The waitress nodded and Tom added. "We'll have a bottle of the house white, medium dry."

"I think there is something you should know about me, Tom," Paula said, as the girl went away. "About money and me." She faced him frankly across the table. "I don't have any."

Tom threw up his hands. "That's us washing dishes."

"No, seriously," she said. "I have enough to pay for this holiday and to live comfortably in the future." She smiled at the word 'comfortably'. "But I am not rich, not in the way Herbie seems to think I am. Neither is Rose. We are not in any position to finance one of his films."

"I wouldn't worry. Herbie works in mysterious ways."

"It's Rose really," she went on. "Rose is taken up with all this film business. Actors, Producers, Directors - it all seems so glamorous to her and I suppose she doesn't want to put Herbie straight just yet."

"And you? Don't you like the movies?"

"Oh yes," she said. "I love films, especially the old films, and I like being here. It is all very glamorous, but I don't like to mislead people. So I thought you ought to know, that's all. I mean, if you were under the same impression as Herbie then I'm glad I've told you. So what do you think of that?"

"Well," he said carefully, "as you like the movies, and especially the old movies, I can offer you a choice." He was an excellent mimic and Paula recognised Gable and Bogart at once. "You can have, 'Frankly, my dear, I don't give a damn.' Or you can have, 'Paula! This could be the start of a beautiful friendship.' "

Paula laughed and clasped her hands in delight. "And you really don't mind?"

"Of course not," he said. "I'm relieved. At least,

you know I'm not after your money."

Paula leaned across the small round table, her chin resting on her upturned hand. "Then what are you after?"

"Your body. Your comfortable body, of course."

The young waitress overheard as she arrived to take their orders. Pretending to be shocked, she raised her eyebrows theatrically and murmured, "*M'sieur*!"

Back at the hotel Herbie and Rose were in the lobby. They'd had a lovely morning, Rose said. They'd been to see a private showing of a British film that was up for a prize. Then they'd had lunch at a little restaurant on the old quay.

Herbie had arranged for Tom to make up a four at tennis with a director friend, the director's wife and their teenage daughter. Herbie wanted the man to direct the film he was hoping to produce. So let him win, he ordered. Tom made a face at Paula and she wondered what hold Herbie had over him.

"Why don't you make up your own fours?" Paula asked, in Tom's defence.

"What him?" Rose laughed and opened Herbie's jacket. "Have you seen this barrel he carries around?"

It appeared that Jim the producer had not been well that morning and someone asked how he was. Herbie said the old boy was resting.

"He's a funny man," Paula said, meaning odd. "All he does is glare at people."

"Ah yes," Tom explained, with a laugh. "Result of a stroke. The way Edina tells it he developed that look to put people off asking for more money. Then one day someone did, he had a mild stroke and the look stuck."

"You like him, don't you?" Paula said.

"I love them both. They're extraordinary people, Paula. Trouble is, they're great jokers. You never know what they'll do next."

"Now listen," Herbie cut in. "We're going into Nice tonight. Dinner at the Chantecler, guests of a Saudi gentleman. Tom and I will pick you ladies up here, in the lobby, about seven. If that's okay."

Tom nodded and looked at Paula and Paula didn't demur. Then Tom went off to change for his game of tennis and Herbie walked Rose and Paula to the lift.

"Colombe d'Or, huh?" he said to Paula, evidently impressed. "That's the place you take your best girl."

In the bedroom Rose took off her shoes and fell back on the bed. Paula went out to the balcony, not admitting it to herself but scanning the seafront in the hope of catching a glimpse of Tom who was walking back to where he was staying. She had only that morning realised he was not staying at the hotel. Someone had loaned him an apartment.

"He likes you, doesn't he?"

"Who?" Paula asked, blushing slightly.

"Tom, of course. You can see it a mile off."

"He's just on his own, that's all. Lonely, perhaps."

"Lonely? What here? With all this going on?"

"He seems to want to get away from all this."

"Well, he's probably seen it all before. They all have. It's just business to them. This fella tonight, this Sheik something or other. Herbie only wants him to finance his film."

"Then shouldn't Herbie be doing the inviting?"

"Nah! You don't worry about who's paying. These Arabs have got pots of money. It's coming out of their ears. All that black stuff. It's called oil."

"You soon catch on, Rose."

"Well, it's your fault. You taught me how to be a free-loader an' it's easy when you know how."

"You're not a free-loader, Rose Parker. You're my friend and confidante. Herbie Kay and Co are the free-loaders."

"Then what are we?"

"We're their fancy women," Paula said and they fell about laughing.

"So what about Tom?" Rose asked when the hilarity subsided.

"What about him?"

"Well, he's a bit of a mystery man you have to admit. Good-lookin' fella like him." She made a face. "Lonely?"

"He's a screen-writer."

"And what else? Is he married? Separated? Divorced? Ask him. Is he or has he ever been married? And the thing is with this lot - how many times?"

"You sound like one of those interrogators on American TV. 'Are you or have you ever been a member of the Communist Party?' "

"What?" Rose was lost. "A Communist? I thought all that stuff was finished."

"Forget it, Rose," Paula said gently. "I'm sure Tom isn't a Communist."

Paula had taken off her blazer. She hauled the blue dress over her head, kicked off her shoes and lay back on her bed. It was true she didn't really know anything about Tom. She'd been too full of her own affairs. She'd probably talked too much about Ted, her husband, and how it felt to lose him. She'd probably been a bore. Next time they were alone she would ask him about himself - if only out of politeness, she deluded herself.

The truth was she was curious now and she couldn't wait to discover more about him.

Rose was out on the balcony. Paula sat up. The breakfast trolley had gone but the rose, the single red rose, was on the dressing table. Again she wondered who could possibly have sent it. Tom had made no mention of it, not even when they walked through the rose garden in St Paul. She picked up her dressing gown from the foot of the bed and found the crumpled note in the pocket. 'To Mrs Blossom, the loveliest lady in the whole of Cannes.' Bit of an exaggeration, Paula reflected. Right over the top! But who could it be? Some short-sighted old codger, no doubt. Jim, perhaps? He seemed to like her, if the way he glared at her was anything to go by.

"Hiya, cock!" Rose was calling to the actress Arlene, who was shaking out a bikini on a balcony lower down. "On your own? Come on up."

"Now?" Arlene asked.

"Yeah, come on. There's just me an' Paula. An' no men, thank goodness. We're just having a natter."

"I'll be right up."

"Who are you talking to?" Paula asked.

Rose came inside. "It's Arlene. She's coming up."

Paula lay back on the bed. No need to get up. No dress, no shoes. Just a cool slip. She felt ... comfortable. She laughed again at the word and Rose cocked an eyebrow at her.

"It's nothing," Paula told her. "It's just something Tom said."

"He's good for you, that fella. Do you know that? I haven't seen you laugh so much for ages."

There was a brisk tap at the door and Arlene came

in with three glasses and a bottle of chilled Moet. "A secret meeting of the All-British Bubbly Club."

"All-British?" Paula queried.

"Oh, yes," Arlene said. "I was born in Brighton. I didn't go to the States until I was twelve."

"Where do you live now?" Rose asked, blunt as ever.

"Anywhere, kid. I took my last husband for all he was worth so I can afford to live wherever I want to. I broke him up and I have no regrets. It's not that I'm hard. It's just that he deserved it - the bastard."

She laughed and popped open the champagne.

"Are you going to go on working?" Paula asked.

"I hope so," Arlene admitted. "But my last picture really bombed. It was set in the Phillippines - or it was supposed to be. It was actually shot in Puerto Rico. It cost more than old man Marcos screwed out of Manila and it still bombed. So now I'm looking for a nice little low budget movie that actually pays its way or, at least, breaks even. I can't afford another bomb."

Rose held up her glass by the long stem. "To nice little low budget movies that actually pay their way."

"I'll drink to that," Arlene said.

"Are you coming into Nice with us tonight?" Paula asked.

"God, no!" Arlene said. "We met the sheik last night."

"Is he a real sheik?" Rose asked.

"Oh sure," Arlene said, "and he's a real pain in the ass, too." They spluttered over their champagne. Encouraged, Arlene went on, "You have to watch him, girls. He'll have you in his tent before you're through salami-ing, as Herbie calls it. And watch his hands. He's like a goddam octopus. He's got so many folds in this kimono he wears you can never tell where the next attack is coming from."

"I'll flatten the bugger!" Rose threatened.

Paula laughed. "So what happened to poor Phillipe?" she asked, changing the subject.

"I don't know," Arlene said. "Laura and I saw him mooching along the Croisette on our way back here but when he saw us he went off up a side street."

"Should we know him?" Paula frowned. "I mean, what has he been in?"

Arlene shook her head. "I don't think so. He's done a lot of French films. In fact, he was in one with Truffaut as a kid. And he's made a few Spaghetti Westerns. That's how he met Nina."

"I can't imagine Phillipe as a cowboy," Rose said, with a laugh. "I should think he wouldn't know his horse from his elbow."

"He's quite a good rider," Arlene said, in his defence. "But he always plays the sort of pretty boy baddy."

"He's pretty, all right," Rose conceded.

"And he's so fond of Nina," Paula said. "It's sad really. I thought they looked lovely together until that Marvyn what's-his-name came between them."

"Brodsky," Arlene said distastefully. "Marvyn Brodsky. Got a lot of pull on both sides of the pond." And she added, for the benefit of Rose's puzzled brow, "The Atlantic. Plenty of girls waiting to jump into bed with him."

"I couldn't ever do that," Paula said. "I mean, it's a form of prostitution."

"If you've ever been really poor and desperate to get on ..." Arlene's voice trailed.

"Course you could," Rose said throatily. "It's like Herbie says, in this business you gotta screw them when they think they're screwing you."

"Rose! You're getting to sound as bad as they are."

"She's right, Paula," Arlene said. "In the beginning, for a lot of girls, their body is all they have." She shrugged. "If they want the big prizes ..."

"It would have to be a very big prize to get me into bed with Marvyn Brodsky," Paula told her. "And he'd have to wear a big bag over his head for a start."

They laughed at Paula's obviously heart-felt sincerity and Arlene drained what was left of the champagne into their glasses.

"The thing is with Nina," Arlene attempted to explain, "she's made mostly French films up to now. I know she's Italian but nearly all her work has been with small-time French directors. What she wants is Hollywood. And as our friend Herbie also says, 'Nina had to kiss a lot of frogs before she landed this prince.' "

"Frogs as in French?" Rose cut in. "Hey, that's good."

"Brodsky?" Paula queried. "A prince?"

"Prince of Hollywood, Paula," Arlene insisted.

"Well, I think it's a shame," Paula said. "I think Nina will regret it. And I think she'll lose Phillipe."

Rose laughed. "She'll probably lose Phillipe anyway. I bet he'd sleep with Brodsky if he thought there was something in it for him."

"Well, ye-es." To Rose's surprise Arlene agreed. "I'd say there's probably more truth in that than you think. But this is a little different. Phillipe really is smitten with Nina. I understand there was trouble in Venice. Some Italian cameraman made a pass at her or said something he shouldn't and Phillipe went berserk. Broke the guy's camera over his head and pushed him into the canal. The guy pressed charges and they're still awaiting the outcome. I understand he really was violent - no kidding - and from the look on his face last night I'd say he was in that sort of mood."

"Well, why not?" Rose said. "This fella Brodsky is a real shit. Everybody thinks so." She glanced at Paula. "Sorry, my love. Mr Brodsky is not a very nice man."

They were out on the balcony now. Below and to the right the flags of several nations flapped above the main hotel entrance. Beyond the palm trees the Mediterranean lay, as far as the eye could see, like a slate blue desert in the afternoon sun.

"There's your boyfriend," Rose said, pointing towards a small group in tennis whites, racquets in cases held loosely or clamped under their arms.

Paula saw Tom. A girl of no more than sixteen was hanging on to his free arm.

"Another hit," Arlene said indulgently. "Absolutely smitten. Head over heels, as they used to say."

Paula looked at her, disconcerted.

"She's a nice kid," Arlene went on, "and her parents are the nicest people you could wish to meet. He's a damned fine director, top class and I mean class. And he's only had the one wife, which is quite something with this crowd. Devoted to them both - mother and daughter. I'd say Tom Daniels is just about the only man he'd trust with the girl - or with his wife, for that matter. Even in a game of tennis."

They watched as the director, his wife and daughter left Tom on the forecourt, both the wife and the girl reaching up to kiss him on the cheek, the wife lightly, the girl with much more abandon, both arms about his neck. Tom turned as they came inside under the awning, raised a hand then walked off alone along the Croisette, smashing the breeze with his covered racquet, behaving more like a young man of eighteen than a world-weary screen-writer in his fifties.

"Do you know Tom well, Arlene?" Paula asked.

"I've never worked with him," Arlene said, "but he has a pretty good reputation. He's more a sort of script doctor than a writer. If there's something wrong with a script, and there usually is, most people want someone like Tom to fix it. I think people like him for his honesty. They know he can do the job and they also know that if it's a lousy script he'll say so and hand it back. But you can bet if there's something in there, something worth finding, Tom'll find it."

Paula was about to ask if he had ever been married but she decided to save that question for Tom himself.

"Has he ever been married?" Rose asked.

"I don't know," Arlene said. "He may have been, I suppose, but not for as long as I've known him and I've known him for ... oh, twenty years or so."

"A girl on every set or whatever you call 'em, eh?"

"I don't know, Rose. I don't know what he was like with other girls. But once - I must have been about thirty, thirty two - we were at the Venice festival and my first husband, the bastard, had to fly to Paris and stay over. The Lido was full of film people and my husband, the bastard, asked Tom to take care of me - which he did beautifully. He took me to the Cipriani."

"What's that?" Rose asked.

"Only one of the best hotel restaurants in the world," Arlene told her. "Anyway, he took me to the Cipriani for dinner. He talked to me. He treated me like a lady, for God's sake. And he told me things about the film business from the inside, things he had learned the hard way. But best of all, he made me laugh. Then he paid the bill and took me back to my hotel. Just the two of us in this goddam water taxi!" She smiled, basking in the recollection. "Then he kissed my hand and said good night."

"And if he'd said let's hit the hay, you'd have said step this way."

"Rose," Paula said .

"Just practising my American accent," Rose said.

Together they turned to Arlene. "Well?"

"It would have been a near thing," Arlene confessed. "But he didn't. Mind you, if I'd known then what I know now about my ex-husband, the bastard, I'd probably have dragged Tom into bed myself."

"But why didn't he?" Rose persisted. "A beautiful girl like you. You must have been stunning in those days."

"Thank you, Rose," Arlene said, with a grimace.

"I mean, you still are. But you know what I mean. The question is, why didn't he?"

"Perhaps he's a gentleman," Paula said reasonably. "He was supposed to be taking care of a friend's wife."

"Or maybe he prefers men," Rose suggested.

Arlene laughed and shook her head as if there was absolutely no question. "Oh no," she said, "not Tom. And I'm sure there are plenty of ladies around the world who would happily testify to that effect."

"Look there!" Rose suddenly pointed to a solitary figure in a crumpled dinner jacket, black tie hanging loose. He was trudging along the Croisette, his mane of jet-black hair curling over his upturned collar. "It's Phillipe!"

"So it is," Arlene said. "Poor boy. I hope he's calmed down a bit. The way he was last night he could have murdered Marvyn Brodsky."

Chapter Five

Paula examined her face in the dressing table mirror. It was a little puffy around the eyes and her skin looked dry. She was not used to this all systems go life style and the cracks were beginning to show. She smiled ruefully. She would have to snatch a siesta here and there. But it was not so much the physical toll that concerned her. She was searching for signs of ... what? Guilt?

Guilt because she had enjoyed her morning with the screen-writer so much? All they had done was talk and laugh and have lunch. And briefly, on the way back to the car, their hands had touched. So why guilt? A mild flirtation was all it was. It didn't constitute a betrayal, for goodness sake! But it was too soon. Ted had only been dead a few weeks and she was strolling hand in hand in the South of France with a man she had only just met.

It was all Ted's fault anyway. The holiday was his idea. Paula took his photograph from her suitcase and propped it up on the dressing table before her. The laughing eyes, the greying hair, the lips where nearly always a smile lay in wait - he was part of her and had been for more than half her life. "Oh, Ted," she said. "Ted!"

Paula hadn't heard Rose come in from the bathroom. Now, in the mirror, she saw her standing there, her hair piled high, her face glistening with cream, a towel wrapped around her still slim body. Rose had noticed the photograph of Ted, sensed her friend's mood. She put a hand on Paula's shoulder. Paula looked back at her and smiled.

"You all right?"

Paula nodded. "I've just been telling Ted it's another fine mess he's got me into."

Rose shook her head. "It's not Ted. It's Tom. You're falling for him, aren't you?"

Paula didn't deny it. She simply changed the subject. "Listen," she said briskly. "We can't go on like this. We're going to have to put something on ourselves."

"How do you mean?"

"Well, we can't accept all this hospitality without paying for anything. I think we should hold a dinner party, invite them all."

"It'd cost a bomb."

"It's the least we can do, Rose, and we can afford it."

That evening Tom Daniels arrived early at the Carlton bar. He knew Herbie Kay would be there and he wanted to talk to him before they got caught up in his entourage. Even so there was a young man at Herbie's elbow. The young man, dark-eyed and sharp featured, was from a New York showbiz magazine and Tom knew him slightly. Tom took Herbie by the arm and told the journalist, "I'm sorry but I have to talk to Mr Kay privately."

The young man looked hurt.

"It's private business," Tom said. "Confidential."

"Gimme a break," the young man persisted. "That's what I'm here for."

"Not this, you're not."

Tom propelled the cigar-wielding Herbie to a small table aware he had created a wound he would later, for professional reasons, need to heal. The young man lingered at the bar, like a child excluded from a game.

"Their circulation is going up, Tom," Herbie warned, referring to the magazine the young man represented.

"Your circulation will go up when I tell you what I heard today," Tom told him as they sat down.

"What?" Herbie demanded. "What's up?"

"Your game with the two 'angels' from England."

"How do you mean?"

"I had lunch with Paula."

Herbie nodded knowingly. "So I heard."

"She told me you're wasting your time if you think she's loaded. She's no more 'mega-rich' than I am. Neither is Rose."

Herbie merely smiled. "I know that's Paula's story. But Rose tells it different. Paula likes you, Tom. She just wants to know if you're after her money."

"She hasn't got any money."

"You should talk to Rose," Herbie said, with a complacent grin. "She'll put you right."

Arlene had arrived, early for once, and the young man from the magazine was telling her how gorgeous she looked. Arlene's escort for the evening was the short, fat, white-haired man who seemed to know everybody at the festival who was anybody and quite possibly did. He was the Hollywood-based agent for many well known actors, including Arlene and Laura, and many not so well-known but equally profitable directors, writers, musicians and other technicians. He even had a couple of legendary songwriters on his books. But right now he was at the bar, asking in sign language what Tom and Herbie were drinking and trying, like a dozen or more others, to catch the waiter's eye.

They went over and joined him just as Jim and his wife Edina arrived.

The young journalist turned to Tom. "I reckon this is the last but one stop for you, eh Tom? If things don't pan out here it's the end of the road, huh? Hacksville."

Tom ignored the over familiarity and smiled sweetly. "I don't think so, son. I wouldn't want to live in the same town as you."

"I've been trying to get Tom to do an original for me," Arlene said, having overheard the exchange. She slipped an arm through Tom's and gazed up at him, soft-eyed and adoring. "But I'm afraid there's no chance of that. They're queueing up for his services here. He's had at least three offers to my knowledge."

With a sardonic smile the young journalist drifted away and attached himself to the fringe of another group.

"Did I ever tell you how much I love you?" Tom said and, just as Paula and Rose arrived, he kissed Arlene lightly on the cheek.

"Unfortunately no," Arlene told him. "And anyway, here's your date."

Paula and Rose, refreshed by their siesta, were glowing. Paula wore a sleek black dress that complemented her short blonde hair. Rose, in dark haired contrast, looked remarkably chic in a beautifully tailored green and gold two piece suit. Heads turned as they entered. Herbie Kay was visibly impressed. "Rosie," he gushed, "you look stunning."

"I do, don't I?" Rose agreed happily.

"You, too, Paula," Herbie added.

Seeing Arlene and Tom together Paula felt she had been mistaken to consider herself a contender. Arlene was just so beautiful - and even if Arlene wasn't interested in Tom several of the younger women obviously were. It was quite unfair, Paula concluded. A man could walk around with a much younger woman on his arm, especially here, and sometimes it was carried to extremes as with Marvyn Brodsky, who was at least sixty, and Nina, who was about twenty two. But even this seemed more acceptable than vice versa. A woman of sixty with a twenty two year old boy was invariably his grandmother.

Arlene and her escort, the Hollywood agent whose name was Lefty Lamar, were going to a different party and as the others assembled, ready to leave, they took to the high stools at the bar.

"Watch out for the whirling dervish!" Arlene called to Paula and Rose.

"What's a whirling dervish?" Rose asked as they made their way to the forecourt.

"I think it's an Arab who does a weird dance and sort of flings his arms about," Paula offered.

"No way to speak of our host," Edina said huffily.

By now both Paula and Rose were wary of a lecherous sheik in flowing robes whom they had not yet met. But at the Hotel Negresco in Nice when they were led to a small reception room adjacent to the internationally famous Chantecler Restaurant, a suavely handsome man in black tie and white dinner jacket came forward to greet them. He kissed the ladies' hands and slapped the gentlemen lightly and affectionately on their backs, offering cigarettes from a solid gold case.

"Still smoking, Bondi," Edina commented.

"I know, my dear. I am smoking a death sentence. But if the cigarettes don't get me something else will."

The exchange was dead and the sheik wanted it buried but Edina was set to continue. Diplomatically Herbie changed the subject.

"Bondi now has a chain of cinemas to his name," he announced to no one in particular.

"How's that?" Jim glared at the sheik.

Bondi shrugged dismissively. "It's just business."

A long thin waiter, silent as a shadow, indicated that the table in the restaurant was ready. Bondi smiled and nodded and the party moved slowly from the small private room on the fringe of the magnificent Negresco ballroom to the intimate dining room graced in the past by so many luminaries.

Rose gave Paula a little dig in the ribs. "Beats scrubbin' your kitchen floor," she murmured.

Paula laughed and Herbie looked back with raised eyebrows. "We were just saying," Paula explained. "If our friends could see us now..."

The restaurant manager danced attendance, greeting the sheik with what looked like genuine warmth and soon the party for dinner were seated at a large table and Herbie Kay was holding forth. He spoke openly of his plans for a new project and this puzzled Paula. Wasn't it all supposed to be confidential at this stage?

Paula, not surprisingly as she had engineered the move herself, was sitting next to Tom. She felt safe with Tom, protected and able to relax. Comfortable. She smiled wryly to herself. That word was cropping up a little too often.

Tom anticipated her question. "With a man like Bondi," he whispered so only she could hear, "you have to be open. Tell him what's on your mind from the start."

The wine was beginning to flow. Mentally Paula went

over what she had consumed that day. She'd had wine at lunch at the Colombe d'Or. She'd shared a bottle of Moet with the girls. She'd had a couple of cocktails, one at the Carlton and one here. She was simply not accustomed to it and now the mere thought of more wine made her feel quite light-headed.

Rose was between Tom and Herbie. Paula stretched across Tom, her hand somewhat familiarly in his lap, and whispered, "Tell Herbie what we said. You know, about the meal."

"Are you sure?" Rose asked, also in a whisper. "Can't we wait until we're in a Macdonald's or somewhere?"

"Go on. Tell him," Paula prompted.

Rose realised that Paula was a little tipsy. She also realised that if Paula offered to pay for the meal Herbie would be even more convinced she really could afford to be an 'angel'. And that would mean the party would be far from over. And Rose didn't want the party to be over. She had never had so much fun in her whole life.

"I don't think the sheik would even consider such a thing," was Herbie's initial reaction. But then it occurred to him that such a show of affluence would imply that he really did have other irons in the fire and he repeated, rather more loudly, "As I was saying, I'm sure our host would not permit such a thing."

The sheik raised his thick black eyebrows. "Am I to know what I would not permit?"

Herbie hunched his shoulders apologetically. "You must forgive me, Bondi. I wouldn't want you to take this the wrong way but our good friends here, the ladies from England, they tell me they are so pleased to have made your acquaintance that as a ... a gesture of goodwill and ... and friendship..." He was floundering. "With your permission, of course. They would like to pay for this evening's dinner."

Tom looked at Herbie as if Herbie was out of his mind but the sheik merely nodded and smiled.

"What do you think, Bondi?" Rose asked. "I mean, no offence like."

The sheik leaned across the table and covered Rose's hand with his own. "No offence, my dear. If you wish, you pay."

Tom glanced at Paula and Paula, despite being light-headed, realised this had just negated the confession she had made to him at lunch.

The dinner progressed with Rose instructing Herbie to choose only the finest wines - which, to Rose, meant the most expensive - and afterwards a round of liqueurs for the ladies and brandy and cigars for the men.

Jim, the extinct producer, glared at the cigar box but took one, rejected the head waiter's offer to trim it for him and popped it into his breast pocket.

The head waiter lit the long brown Havanas and the chef de cuisine appeared for his deserved but expected plaudits. Then the sheik put his hands on the table and, cigar gripped between his nicotine-stained teeth, again leaned across towards Rose.

"I have enjoyed your company so much," he told her.

"I thought you Arabs liked fat women," Rose replied, losing her posh accent. "Y'know, bit o' meat on 'em."

For the others present there was a moment of consternation but the sheik merely laughed. "We Arabs," he said, "like many things. Especially Western women."

"Bondi went to Eton," Herbie said lamely.

Rose opened her mouth but Paula threw her a look and, despite the fact that Paula's hair had fallen over one eye and her movements were becoming progressively less precise, something in that look served to restrain her.

"I think you are absolutely charming, Bondi," Rose said, posh again and a little tipsy herself by now.

"For an Arab?" Bondi suggested with a smile.

"I mean it. That Rudolph Valentino had nowt on you."

The sheik looked puzzled for a moment then he said softly, "I was about to make you an offer."

"Ooh!" Rose responded.

"Perhaps I should say a request." He reached out and touched her hand. "I have enjoyed this evening so much," he went on, "I can only accept your proposal to pay for it with the greatest reluctance. Please allow me to - how you say? - toss you for it."

"What?" Rose withdrew her hand.

"We toss a coin."

"Oh, right!" Rose said. "Heads I win, tails you lose."

"Herbie," the sheik said. "A coin, please."

Herbie balanced a coin on his thumb and Bondi indicated that Rose should call.

"Tails!" she chose.

And before anyone had an opportunity to witness the result the sheik had scooped the coin from the back of Herbie's hand. "Tails it is," he announced with an expansive smile. "The lady wins, so I pay!"

He drew the black evening dress up to around her waist then he saw he would have to release a small clasp in the nape of her neck. To make it easier for him, Paula put her forehead against the lapel of his dinner jacket. The room swayed like the deck of an unstablised steamer in a storm and she knew she was well and truly drunk.

The wine at dinner had finally tipped her over the edge and she was only vaguely aware of her surroundings. Yet she knew with absolute clarity that she was with Tom and they were alone and he was slowly and carefully undressing her. What's more, she didn't want him to stop.

He drew the dress up and over her head and she clung to him, her bare arms about his neck. She wanted him to kiss her fully and passionately on the lips but he simply eased her gently back on to the bed, then he straightened up and removed his jacket and tie.

Paula lay back on the soft cover, her arms spread, inviting him to join her but he sat on the edge, removed her underskirt and deftly drew down her thin-meshed tights.

She closed her eyes but the turbulence increased. It was like being on a roller coaster in the dark with no guarantee that the ride would soon be over. She gave out an involuntary groan and, drunk as she was, she felt embarrassed. Tom made her sit up.

"I feel sick," she said.

She gagged, stood up and Tom helped her swiftly to the bathroom. Four times she bowed her head over the toilet bowl and each time she brought up a substantial part of what she had eaten earlier. She was mortified, ashamed, and she wished Tom would go away.

The sight of her, she thought glumly, kneeling here in her pants and bra, making these dreadful retching noises, her make-up all blurred, her hair a mess, must surely have extinguished any faint kindling of romance there might have been between them.

"Go on, Paula," Tom said. "You'll feel better for it, I promise you." He patted her lightly on the top of her head - which seemed like a final indignity - and went back into the bedroom.

Her humiliation was complete. His quiet encouragement had only made her feel worse. Getting drunk, unable to conduct herself - what must he think of her? For a third time she flushed the toilet, vowing vehemently she would never touch a drop of alcohol for the rest of her life.

She washed her hands under the running tap then filled the basin with cold water and splashed her face. There was a large mirror on the wall to her right. She examined her reflection. She was pale - like the Ghost of Christmas Past, she thought irrelevantly - but she was pleased to see she didn't look anything like as bad as she felt.

Tom came to the bathroom door, put an arm around her shoulders and steered her back to bed.

"So tell me, Mr Screen-writer," she said, blowing a wayward strand of hair from her eyes, "what on earth did you see in me?"

"Style," he said. "You have style and a touch of class."

"Style?"

"The way you wear your hat," he said. "The way you sip your tea."

"I don't wear a hat and I drink coffee."

"You know what I mean," he said. "And speaking of coffee..." There was a cup of black coffee on the bedside table. He smiled and said, "You should take a couple of aspirins or something."

Paula reached for her bag. With every move she made the room still swayed and her hand shook disconcertingly as she searched for the aspirins. She knew she had been willing to go to bed with Tom earlier in the evening and from the way she had behaved he must have known it, too. But right now there was no way she wanted to engage in anything other than sleep.

She sipped at the coffee and swallowed two aspirins. Already the coffee was lukewarm yet, unpalatable though it was, she consumed it all. She would have to find the bathroom again before long anyway. What a mess, she thought. What must he think of her? But she was in no condition to agonise over such questions. Like a rag doll, she allowed him to draw her partly to her feet, pull down the covers and put her to bed.

She closed her eyes, wanting to sleep if only to escape the unstable room. But she couldn't. In a confusion that kept her awake, thoughts, feelings, memories from the distant past, recollections of events earlier that evening flooded in.

Occasionally, she recalled, she'd been a little light-headed but very rarely and it was years and years since she'd actually been drunk. She could only remember a couple of times and both of those were when she was just a girl. Once at college she'd been drunk and horribly sick but so had most of the other girls. And there was once when she'd gone to a rugby club dinner with a boy she barely knew and something had almost happened in the back of his father's car. But all that was years ago and she couldn't even remember the boy's name. Now, when she had hoped something would actually happen, when she'd been fully prepared to allow it to happen she'd been in no fit state.

Yet throughout her random meanderings one single, inescapable thought remained. Tom had helped her to undress. In fact, he had undressed her. Then he had put her to bed and put out the light. And he had left her alone.

She was glad he had left her alone - if they were going to do anything together she wanted to be there when it happened, she told herself - but she wondered why he had. A defenceless woman, almost naked, in his bed - what sort of man was he? A gentleman, perhaps. Or perhaps he just didn't fancy her any more. Perhaps her drunken state had simply put him off.

When she opened her eyes Paula turned to glance at the next bed, looking instinctively for Rose. But there was no next bed. This was not their room at the Carlton. It was a strange room and a strange bed and she had slept the night away.

She drew herself up to a sitting position on the edge of the bed and at that moment she felt as though a Sumo wrestler had suddenly sat on her head. Carefully, as if walking on broken glass, she made her way to the bathroom.

Her face was a mess of smudged lipstick and eye shadow, her hair tousled over one eye. She washed away the war-paint, as Rose called it, then gripped the edge of the wash basin to steady herself as she had the night before.

She pulled out her bra and looked inside. Then she did the same with her briefs, not knowing what she expected to find there. Reassured, yet with mixed feelings, she knew she had not been tampered with in any way. Without thinking, she flushed the toilet then realised at once that this might alert Tom who, presumably, had slept elsewhere. She opened the bathroom door slightly, looked around the bedroom.

The black evening dress, her tights and her underskirt were on a chair. Her high-heeled shoes stood neatly side by side. She dressed quickly, drew back the curtains and straightened out the bedclothes. From the single indent on the pillows it was obvious she had slept alone. Once again she didn't know whether to feel glad or sorry.

The bedroom window looked out on to other four or five storey blocks. About three floors down there was a small enclosed yard. Pale-faced, dressed incongruously for the time of day in high heels and the black evening dress, Paula teetered over to the bedroom door, her only escape route.

She opened the door an inch or so, then further. The living room was small, comfortable-looking, and it was nicely furnished with rows of books along one wall. But what claimed her attention was the sofa where a pillow and a neatly folded blanket lay. The open door to a kitchen was on her right. On her left was a door which, she hoped, was the front door, her way out.

Straight ahead was the sliding window to a balcony. It was partly open and Paula got the impression that Tom was out there. She panicked. She didn't want to see him and she didn't want him to see her.

Quietly she crept to the door, let herself out and found she was in a hallway. There was a lift close by, but she couldn't wait. She ran for the stairs.

Out in the street Paula had no idea where she was. If she could find a taxi there would be no problem, she told herself. But she was in a back street and it was nine o'clock in the morning. She hurried to the corner, saw the slate grey sea through gently swaying palm fronds and, reassured, prayed she was within walking distance of the hotel.

She started to walk down to the Croisette, passed some empty tennis courts. A couple of girls in mini skirts and high boots stopped talking to stare at her. If it hadn't been so early in the day she would have guessed they were prostitutes and from the way they were looking at her she feared they thought that she was one, too. Perhaps they thought she'd been poaching their territory.

Fortunately, ahead and to the right, loomed one of the Carlton's impressive blue domes. What she wanted now was to avoid the main entrance and somehow get up to her room without being seen. Unfortunately, she would have to ask for her key at the desk.

She felt haggard and drawn - hungover was the word - and she was convinced she looked a mess. The black dress was crinkled and creased and to make things worse one leg of her tights had sprung a large hole and laddered above and below it.

Her head down, she entered the hotel by a side door, found her way to the front lobby and scuttled over to the desk. Why did it have to be the nice-looking one on duty? He smiled, affable and courteous as always, and said the key was out. Paula thanked him through gritted teeth. So Rose was in. She could have gone straight up.

"Paula!" It was the Italian girl Nina. "Paula, you mus' keese me congratulations! I am so 'appy."

"Are you dear?" Paula responded quietly, glancing

beyond Nina to see who was around.

"I get to be beeg, beeg star! Marvyn is put me in beeg peecture. I leaf for 'ollywood Friday. I am girl in gang banging with three killers on run from preeson."

Paula didn't want to know. "What about Phillipe?" she asked. "Is he going, too?"

"Pah!" The Italian girl pouted her large, voluptuous lips. "*Quel bambino*! I no want to see heem!"

Across the lobby, with several chins squashed on his chest and looking like an overweight satyr, Marvyn Brodsky had appeared.

"Good luck, Nina, whatever you do," Paula said and she turned to head for the stairs. But just then the lift doors opened and Arlene emerged, accompanied by Laura Baker. They looked fresh and bright, ready for a late breakfast.

Arlene took in the situation at once. "Are you just going out or just coming in?"

"Who's been on the tiles then?" Laura asked, equally amused.

"All right, all right," Paula gave up all hope of escape. "I've been out all night and I've got the headache to prove it."

"Water," Arlene suggested. "Lots of it."

"I don't think I could face another drink ever again. Not even water." She displayed the hole in her tights. "I feel as though I've been in a fight."

"I was about to ask," Laura said, with a mischievous grin. "How's the other fella?"

Arlene smiled sweetly. "Tom will be fine."

"Look," Paula said decisively. "I must go. I want to have a shower, get changed. I'll see you girls later."

Barely concealing their amusement, Arlene and

Laura turned to let her go. "Now if it was Rose who'd been out all night ..." Laura's voice trailed.

"Don't you believe it," Arlene said. "Beneath that prim little exterior you have one of the world's great ravers."

"Careful, Arlene," Paula warned. "Or I might just kick that prim little *pos*terior."

The lift doors opened yet again and as Paula turned to enter the director's wife and her pretty teen-aged daughter emerged.

"Good morning," they greeted her brightly and Paula's embarrassment was complete.

CHAPTER SIX

Paula caught the look on Rose's face. "Don't ask," she said, lifting her dress up and over her head as she swept into the room.

There was a knock at the door almost as Rose closed it. Exasperated, Paula pulled the dress back on. It was a small boy bearing a huge bouquet.

"*Madame* Rose?" the boy asked hopefully.

"Ah!" Rose allowed him in. "On the table, sonny."

The boy was barely bigger than the bouquet. He gazed at Rose like a lost cherub.

"*La table, s'il vous plait,*" Paula said. "*Sur la table.*"

The boy bowed. "*Oui, madame.*"

Rose pressed a note in his hand and he left backwards, bowing and smiling angelically as he went.

"With a face like that," Rose said, "that boy will make a fortune in tips."

Again Paula pulled the dress over her head.

"All this French is getting to you, kid," Rose said, with a laugh. "You can't wait to get undressed."

Herbie Kay came out of the bathroom. "Paula! I'm sorry."

"What is this?" Paula complained, covering herself with the discarded dress. "Piccadilly?"

"I'll go. See you later." Herbie backed away, bowing and smiling like the little cherub as Rose bundled him out.

"For goodness sake," Paula said, "lock the door. Unless you have some other men hidden about the place. In the wardrobe? Under the bed?"

"I've been worried about you. Where've you been?"

"Oh yes? I haven't seen any search parties."

"Well, we knew you'd be all right with Tom."

Paula ignored this.

"Well, were you?" Rose persisted. "All right with Tom?"

"Mind your own business," Paula said.

Rose laughed. "You've got a hangover."

"Well, haven't you? You had your share."

"Oh, sure," Rose admitted. "I had a mouth like a camel's crotch first thing."

"You've got Arabs and camels on the brain."

"That sheik fella! Boogie!"

"Bondi," Paula corrected her.

"Whatever his name is."

"You know his name all right," Paula said accusingly.

Rose laughed again. "Arlene was right, you know. He's all over you. He is like a bloody octopus."

"So what happened?"

"We went to the casino and he bought me a pile of chips. He thinks I'm hilarious. So I play him up a bit. You know, like he says, 'Would you like some chips?' And I say, 'Salt and Vinegar, please'. And he falls about laughing."

"He must be as daft as you," Paula said.

"Anyway, he bought me a pile of chips."

"And you lost the lot."

"No, I didn't. That's just it. Every time I put some down I got more back. I couldn't lose. I damned near trebled what he bought me."

"So what did you do?" Paula asked, interested now.

"Well, to tell you the truth, I got a bit scared. I couldn't see Herbie anywhere and it looked as if I was stuck with the sheik and his bodyguard, that fat fella with the beady eyes. So I did a bunk."

"You did what?"

"I did a bunk. Left. Vamoosed, as they used to say in the movies."

A week ago the word 'movies' would have been alien to Rose's vocabulary. Paula regarded her friend indulgently. "So you just walked out?"

"I didn't want to get stuck with those two. I said I'm going to cash in my chips and then go to the powder room. Well, I mean, old sheiky was still playing and he didn't seem to mind, so I went to the desk and they gave me a great stack of notes.

"Then what did I do? I asked them for a big envelope to put them in, sealed it up and asked the head lad to give the envelope to the sheik with my compliments."

Paula nodded in approval. "I think that was right, Rose. I think you did the right thing."

"Well, it was a lot of money," Rose said ruefully, "but the original stake belonged to him. I was playing for him really. And I didn't want to owe him anything."

"Quite right."

"I mean, he might think he'd bought me or something."

"So that explains the flowers."

Rose went to the table. "Must have cost of a few bob," she murmured, then she picked up the card and burst out laughing. "To my English Rose!" She looked at Paula in disbelief. "I've been called a few things in my time but never a bloody English rose!"

She saw the envelope on the table beside the flowers, the large brown envelope, and recognised it at once. "What's this? How did this come?"

"The boy brought it with the flowers."

Rose opened it and shook the bank notes out on to the table in a cascade, some spilling to the floor. "It's the money, Paula. He's sent it back."

Like a child with an unexpected present, she scooped all the money into a little mound on the carpet, sat cross-legged on a cushion and began to count it.

It was mainly in one hundred and five hundred franc notes and the total came to more than thirty thousand. At about seven point four to the pound, Paula observed. What's that? Rose demanded. Quite a lot, Paula told her and she rummaged in her bag for her pocket calculator.

"Hang on," Paula said. "I think this might need a new battery." They had used the calculator rather a lot in the boutiques to work out the price in pounds of some of the inordinately expensive 'rags', as Rose called them, on offer. "How much? Thirty thousand three hundred francs at seven point four?" Paula prodded the calculator. "I make it four thousand and ninety four."

"Pounds?"

Paula did it again. "Four thousand and ninety four pounds and point five nine four pence to be exact."

"Bloody 'ell!" Rose said.

"What are you going to do with it?"

"I don't know. What do you think?"

"I think you should send it back."

"What if he won't have it back? We can't play pass the bloody parcel all week."

"You mean you want to keep it?"

"Well," Rose spread her hands. "He obviously doesn't need it. And it seems such a shame." She laughed. "I never thought you'd catch me sending back four thousand quid. I mean, four thousand. Just like that."

"It might be different if you needed it."

"Well, I do. In a way. I could buy you that yellow dress. The one you tried on. It was lovely. Went great with your hair."

"My hair's not yellow," Paula said. Then, doubting her assertion, she added, "Is it?"

"You know what I mean," Rose said.

"You couldn't buy that. I wouldn't let you. It was ridiculous. Eight hundred and fifty pounds for a bit of cloth. I could run that up myself at home."

"But you're not at home, Paula. You're here with the fast movers. This is the Carlton in Cannes. This is where all the big nobs hang out, if you'll pardon the expression. You wear what they wear, do what they do."

Paula laughed. "I don't know about that. The way some of these people carry on ..."

"Tell me about last night," Rose said. "Tell me what happened."

"Nothing," Paula said. "Nothing happened."

She refused to talk about it. She was with Tom and that was all she was prepared to say. She didn't tell Rose where she had spent the night and she didn't confess that she, too, had 'done a bunk'.

Paula had noticed him before. Tallish, slim, fair hair and bright blue eyes - he was quite good-looking in a bland sort of way. He was no more than eighteen or nineteen but Paula had noticed him because of the way he looked at her. Several times now, in the bar or on the terrace, she had seen him, sometimes out of the corner of her eye. Always a hopeful little smile played on his lips and he seemed to hover watchfully as if waiting for an opportunity to introduce himself.

She had guessed he was Swedish or Danish, certainly Scandinavian. But when they were finally introduced - by Herbie Kay and then only by accident - he said he was from St Paul.

"St Paul de Vence?" Paula enquired.

"Minnesota," the boy said, as if apologising.

"Nothing wrong with that," Laura Baker told him. "That's where F Scott Fitzgerald came from."

"I'm not a writer, Miss Baker," the boy said. "I'm an actor."

"Not yet, you're not," Herbie said. The waiter on duty that afternoon was out on the terrace and Herbie wanted someone to organise coffee. "Go get the coffee."

"What does he do - that young man?" Paula asked as the boy hurried to the bar. "He seems to be all over the place."

"He's Marvyn Brodsky's gofer," Herbie said.

Paula looked puzzled.

"Gofer this, gofer that," explained Rose, who was into all the jargon.

Paula felt sorry for him. "What's his name?"

"Elmer," Arlene said. "I think."

"Ah, don't worry about him," Herbie said. "Blue-eyed blond beefcakes are a dime a dozen back home."

"In Catford?" Rose asked mischievously.

The boy proved extremely efficient and as a result the waiter came running in to reclaim his territory.

"Mrs Blossom," Elmer said, hovering near. "I must

speak with you."

"With me?"

"Please. It is most important to me."

"I can't think why," Paula said lightly. "I have no influence here."

"It's not that, ma'am," he said, touching her hand. "It's sort of personal."

Herbie Kay jabbed a finger at him. "Do you want one?"

"Sir?" The boy looked startled.

"A coffee." Everyone else had one. "You want a coffee?"

The waiter danced attendance, imperiously awaiting his usurper's decision.

"Er ... no, sir," Elmer said and he knew from Herbie's expression his answer was the right one. "Thank you."

He turned away then looked back and smiled at Paula as he left.

"Made a killing there, kiddo," Rose murmured.

"Don't be silly," Paula said. "I'm old enough to be his mother."

"Grandmother more like," Rose replied and they both laughed.

The venue for dinner that evening was again the Blue Parrot, the restaurant down on the old quay. Paula was ready early. She left Rose in the room and went down to the lobby, hoping to see Tom and explain herself before the others arrived.

Brodsky's boy, Elmer, was standing by the main doors, presumably ready to respond to a call from his master. He saw Paula and hurried over. "Mrs Blossom."

Paula looked up at him absently. Her concern at

that moment was for Tom.

"May I speak with you?"

"Not now, dear," she said, raising a hand to Tom who had just arrived.

The boy looked over his shoulder, saw Tom and discreetly slid away. Smiling, Tom came over and kissed her on the cheek.

"Tom," she said. "I'm so sorry."

"It's okay," he said. "No problem."

"But I was awful. And leaving like that - without a word. What must you think of me?"

"I think you know what I think of you."

"But I was sick. It was disgusting."

"You were drunk." He laughed. "Some of my best friends are drunks."

"I'm not a drunk. You mustn't think that. I mean, if I was a drunk I wouldn't have been so sick."

"Don't worry about it," Tom told her.

"When I didn't hear from you today," she said, "I thought you must have had enough of me."

"I've been working today," he said. "Only just back."

"Working?"

"I've been up to Grasse with Steve. Steve Hogan."

"The one with the wife and daughter? Your tennis friends?"

Tom nodded. "He wants me to do a job for him."

Arlene and Laura Baker emerged from the lift and moments later Rose arrived on Herbie's arm.

Paula turned to Tom. "Friends?"

He smiled. "We were never anything less."

It was a lovely evening, warm and windless, the palm trees as still as the stone columns on the seafront. Everyone chose to walk. Everyone except Jim and

Edina, that is. The elderly stooping Jim and his tall unbending wife took a taxi and were already at the bar when the others arrived.

Edina nudged her husband.

"Wha'? Wha'? What's that?' Jim came to life when she caught his eye. "My treat!" He glared at his assembled friends. "The drinks are on me."

"In that case," Arlene said and she reached for the list of cocktails which was printed on a large shiny cardboard cut-out of a blue parrot. "On this historic occasion..."

"How about a screwball?" Laura suggested.

"What's that then?" Paula was unable to find where it was listed.

"It's a cross between a screwdriver and a snowball."

"I think they named it after Rose," Herbie said, with a grin. "Where is she, anyway?"

"Gone to the Powder Room," Paula told him. "And I'll tell her what you said."

"Or a Wallbanger," Laura went on. "How about a Harvey Wallbanger?"

Paula laughed. "Those always sound vaguely rude."

"Great!" Arlene said. "Harvey Wallbangers - okay?"

Rose returned and took to her stool at the bar.

"How about you, Rose?" Herbie asked. "Fancy a Wallbanger?"

"Yeah, why not!" Rose was enthusiastic. "But I think we should have a drink first."

Thus began an evening of hilarity that was to degenerate briefly into what to most of the onlookers resembled farce. With his usual diplomacy Herbie had gone across to say hello to Marvyn Brodsky who was dining at a table for two with his newest protégé, Nina.

No sooner had he rejoined his friends at the round table than the French actor, Phillipe, loomed menacingly in the entrance to the dining room. Those diners who saw the look on Phillipe's face realised at once that there was trouble afoot and promptly stopped eating to watch.

Above the heads of the seated diners Phillipe's dark eyes scoured the crowded room. He was tall and athletic, and he was apparently struggling with some inner fury. The faces of those nearest to him registered concern if not alarm. The little proprietor, Louis, alerted by his large buxom wife, hurried over to forestall whatever he was about to do. "*M'sieur*?"

Phillipe simply brushed Louis aside and strode between the tables, his careless thigh movement dragging a table-cloth sidelong. Two of the male guests at the table stood up to remonstrate but, oblivious to the disruption he was causing, Phillipe came to a halt only when he reached and confronted Marvyn Brodsky.

"Broad-key!" he mispronounced, in a voice filled with hate. "Get app!"

Herbie Kay laid a steadying touch on Rose's hand. Tom glanced at Paula, eyebrows raised in amused speculation. The others watched open-mouthed - all except Jim who, head down intent on his dinner, hadn't noticed.

"What?" Brodsky growled. "What's this?"

"Get app!"

"Phillipe!" Nina's hands went to her mouth in dismay.

Brodsky threw down his napkin and struggled to his feet and without a moment's hesitation the much younger, much fitter Frenchman hit him hard, breaking his spectacles. Brodsky fell back heavily against the table for two, lost his balance and was powerless as his large body slid beneath it.

Nina screamed and people stood up as Brodsky's false teeth skittered across the tiled floor. Three largish men then rose, at Louis' frantic request for help, to restrain Phillipe and evict him. But somehow Phillipe threw them off and faced Nina.

"You cam wid me now or you forget eet. Stay wid de feelthy peeg."

"Go away!" Nina screamed. "Just go!"

"Okay. If these is what you want."

"Marvyn!" Ignoring Phillipe, she went down on one knee. "Oh, Marvyn!"

"My teeth," Brodsky muttered. One hand covered the gap in his mouth, the other fended off the melodramatic Nina. Then, on his hands and knees, he peered short-sightedly at the floor in search of the missing molars.

The little proprietor wrung his hands. "*Mesdames, mesdemoiselles, messieurs! Je regrette infiniment!*" He turned to Herbie. "*M'sieur* Kay, I am so sorry."

"Not your fault, Louis," Tom assured him. "Don't worry about it."

"*M'sieur* Tom, these 'as nevair 'appened at ma place."

"Forget it, Louis," Herbie said. "Settle down, everybody. Show's over."

"Forget it?" Brodsky almost screamed. "This is something I will never forget and neither will that French bastard. I'll see to it he don't work ever again. He's finished, I tell ya. As of now!"

Herbie, who had never liked Brodsky, saw the glossy white, red-gummed teeth and surreptitiously kicked them sideways under several tables. The teeth, open slightly in a sinister grin, came to a halt beside the chair of a sensitive lady who, attracted by the scrape of the teeth across the tiled floor, looked down and, with a piercing scream, leapt from her chair.

Louis hurried over, snatched up a napkin and retrieved the teeth. "I am so sorry, *madame*."

The woman's husband launched into a tirade in German that poor Louis could only interpret from the man's gestures and facial expressions. Nearby another altercation had begun. Insults were being traded in a language which, according to Herbie who said he knew the two men involved, was Russian.

"What a hoot!" Arlene laughed.

"It's just like a UN peace-keeping conference," someone said.

But gradually order was restored, not so much by Louis as by his more than able wife who went between tables ordering the diners to sit down.

"*Asseyez-vous*!" she commanded. "*Asseyez-vous*!"

And most of the diners did.

Brodsky returned from the men's room now, his teeth in place, his eyes pink and small as he peered towards his table and the anxious Nina.

In passing he scowled in Herbie's direction. Then he came back. "Forget it! I won't ever forget it. I'll have that frog ass-hole if it's the last thing I do."

Rose swapped a grin with Paula then exclaimed loudly in her poshest voice, "I say! What fun!"

Brodsky, at his table, declared the dinner a disaster. He rose to leave, the blue-eyed Elmer in attendance.

"And where were you?" Brodsky demanded. "Ya great fairy! Ya shoulda seen him comin'."

The boy was tight-lipped, knowing it was wiser not to apologise, make excuses or say anything at all.

"Get me outa here," Brodsky ordered, his hand over his mouth as if he expected his teeth to take off again.

"I cam wid you," Nina announced.

Brodsky looked at her with distaste. "You can do what you like, ya little tramp. Go to hell, for all I care."

Nina burst into tears.

"It wasn't her fault, you big bully!" Rose called across the dining room.

"I've had enough of this," Brodsky said and he came back to face Rose. "Who the hell are you, anyway? And what the hell are you doing here?"

"What am I doing here?" Rose stood up, more than his match. "I'm waiting for you to sod off so we can all eat in peace. Where I come from pigs like you stay in their sties. And who am I? I'll tell you who I am. I'm someone who doesn't need you."

There was surprised but approving laughter here and there and even a ripple of applause.

"Oh my...!" Paula murmured. "What has she said now?"

"Nothing I can't go along with," Tom said with a grin as Brodsky stormed from the dining room and out on to quay, the blue eyed Elmer at his heels.

Nina chased after them, calling, "Marvyn! Mr Brodsky!" in between her wails.

As soon as Brodsky had left Herbie Kay collapsed into uncontrolled laughter. "Bloody marvellous!" he cried, mopping his eyes.

Louis didn't know whether to laugh or cry.

"Louis, old son, that was great!" Herbie told him. "Your floor shows are getting better all the time."

"*Comment*?" Louis was doubly perplexed.

The excitement subsided and as the evening progressed two of Tom's screen-writing pals and their much younger partners stopped by on their way out.

"I've been wanting to punch Marvyn Brodsky for years," said the taller of the two.

"Me, too," said the other.

Herbie introduced Paula and Rose as 'my very good friends from England'. The two writers seemed to know everyone else.

"Honoured to meet you ladies," the taller one said, with the exaggerated courtesy of a Southern gentleman.

"Sure are," the other said with the voice of Kermit the frog from the Muppet Show.

"Hey, you do that well!" Rose said spontaneously.

"How's that?" Kermit asked, with a frown, and she realised this was his normal voice.

"It's our first time here," Paula said, helping Rose out, and she smiled at the two young girls.

But neither man introduced his partner and the two girls, slim and shapely in their skimpy dresses, stood to one side, wriggling and giggling like a couple of adolescents. Where they came from or who, if anyone, had sponsored them was anybody's guess but there was obviously no shortage of such bimbos at the festival.

"You sure told that old slag-heap," the Southern gent told Rose. "Didn't she, folks? Eh, Tom?"

"Could'nt have scripted it better," Tom agreed.

"You're a gem, ma'am," Kermit said. "You really are."

"A Rose is a Rose is a Rose," Laura Baker said.

"Hey!" Rose cut in. "Didn't somebody famous say

that?"

"Yeah. Me!" Laura acknowledged. "I just did."

"No, I mean someone clever. Y'know, like a writer."

"Well, thank you, Rose," Laura said, with that quirky, arched eyebrow look that graced her most memorable movie roles.

The Southern gent waved his cigar. "Ah do believe it was Gertrude Steinbeck."

"Nah! You're mistaken," Kermit said. "Wrong quote. It was: 'One perfect rose. Why does he never send me one perfect limousine, do you suppose?'"

"No, no," the Southern gent disagreed. "That was Parker, Lady Penelope's chauffeur."

"I should watch it, boys," Laura warned them. "My friend Rose eats intellectuals for breakfast."

"Are these two taking the mick?" Rose asked.

Laura nodded solemnly. " 'fraid so."

"Right then," Rose told them. "In that case, we'd better say good-night. It's time your little granddaughters were in bed."

The two writers duly chastened and despatched, Rose turned to Herbie Kay. Herbie had decided he wanted to go to a private showing of a new French film, partly because the director was young, busy building a reputation for himself and was not yet wildly expensive.

"I don't want to watch a French film," Rose said. "They're boring."

"I want you to watch it," Herbie told her. "I value your opinion."

"I won't understand a word."

"It's sub-titles."

"Oh, my God! At this time of night?"

"Rose. I want you to see this film. I want you to tell me what you think of it. I want a totally unbiased view."

"And he wants you to go to bed with him afterwards," Arlene chortled.

"That, too," Herbie admitted.

Rose brightened. "Oh, right! In that case..."

For professional reasons Herbie insisted on dragging Tom along, but both Paula and Laura Baker declined his invitation. Paula knew that if she sat through a couple of hours of some turgid sub-titled melodrama, and that, in her experience, is what French films invariably were, she would end up with an almighty headache. Laura said she had seen enough French films, thank you very much, and anyway she wanted to walk back along the seafront in the moonlight. The others had called a cab and were ready to leave. Paula said she would like to walk back, too, get some fresh air.

Laura was glad of Paula's company. "Ladies walking alone at night attract more rats than the Pied Piper," she said. "And at this time of year Cannes has more than its share of rats."

Tom said simply, "See you tomorrow."

And Paula was relieved. She had not yet decided how far she wanted to go with Tom. She was more than merely attracted to him and when she was with him it seemed so right. But she had not been looking for a man. She was not ready, she told herself. She was not sure she would ever be ready. She was not sure she would ever want to be ready. Yet she couldn't help feeling a little disappointed that he had made no attempt to persuade her to stay.

A bright moon glimmered on the dark water and the evening was windless and warm. Along the Croisette there was sporadic laughter, like short bursts of gunfire, and the occasional screech of tyres as someone did a brake start. Here and there, on both sides of the road, shadowy knots of people blocked the pavements and sometimes a lone cigarette glowed beside a darkened wall.

Strolling beside Laura Baker, Paula suddenly laughed. "You'd say I was really boring if I told you what I was thinking just now."

"Try me," Laura said.

"I was thinking: Here am I, plain old Paula Blossom, a very ordinary housewife from a small town in the north of England, strolling along the Croisette in Cannes, one of the most famous promenades in the world, with Laura Baker, one of the most famous ladies in Hollywood."

Laura threw her a look, the arched eyebrow look again, and gave out a coarse, deep throated laugh of derision.

"You're right," she said. "You are boring."

Paula laughed with her but then Laura said, "You know, all that stuff about fame, it doesn't change people. Not unless they're really stupid. I mean, when you're alone you still have all the same old hang-ups and probably a few new ones. Sometimes being famous, which more or less means your face is known to the general public, makes things worse. Not better. You don't change. What does change is the attitude of other people towards you. Oh, I know there are plenty of girls who would say, 'Who are you kidding?' But I can assure you, it's not always pleasant. Quite often you come across people who have decided they don't like you and they've never even met you. Now money, money is different.

"I sometimes think the best of all ways to be is just incredibly rich and totally unknown. And if it came to a choice between money and fame I'd say give me the money every time. Chances are the older you get the more miserable you get. So I reckon it's better to be miserable in comfort, Paula. As Marilyn used to sing, 'We all lose our charms in the end.'"

"For a film star," Paula told her, "you're incredibly down to earth."

Laura laughed. "Boring you mean?"

She was a fascinating woman, thought Paula. Easily the most interesting woman she had ever met. She'd been at the top of her profession now for more than thirty years. A stunningly attractive new face in her earliest films, she had matured into a fine actress with a string of quality roles behind her and even now, in her early sixties, she was still in demand.

Laura Baker had married her first leading man, a world famous actor who was forty seven when she was twenty two. He had died relatively young, after a long illness, just a few years later and, though she had been married briefly in her thirties, she had never got over losing him. Few men could match his charm and his peculiar brand of throw away humour and her second husband, aware from the start of the ghost that stood between them, soon came to realise he had little or no chance of taking his place.

"Laura Baker is one hell of a woman," Tom had told Paula. "She's been just about everywhere, done just about everything, and yet she's still totally straight and unspoilt. No frills, no edge. Just great to be with and still a very good-looking lady. Everybody loves her."

"You sound as though you're half in love with her yourself," Paula had said.

"I probably am," he'd admitted. "Most men who know her are. And I'll tell you something else. Laura has more lady friends than any other woman I know - and that's really something. Tearing each other apart is a matter of routine for most of the women in our business."

"So how goes it with you and Tom?" Laura asked, as if alerted telepathically. "You two getting it together?"

Paula was not sure what she meant. "I like him," she said cautiously. "I like him a lot."

"Well, that's good. Because he's hooked on you."

"You think so?"

"I know so," Laura said. "I've known Tom Daniels a long time now. Thirty years or more. He's a good man, Paula, and you know what they say. A good man is hard to find. He doesn't chase after bits of skirt half his age and he's a long term guy, a good friend to have. If I need some objective advice, a second opinion with no strings, I know that Tom is just a phone call away."

"Have you and he never...?"

Laura shook her head. "He was a friend of my first husband. Or rather his father was. When he was just a kid out of college my husband helped him get a job with the studio. Of course he was nearer my age but my husband trusted him and rightly so. We were just good friends in those days and we've stayed that way."

"Has he never been married?"

"Once. Years ago. He married a young actress, lovely girl, but they were only together a few months before she was killed in an automobile accident."

They had arrived back at the Carlton. Laura turned

to Paula and smiled. "He's a gentleman, Paula. Believe me. The sort of guy you can trust and there aren't too many of those around. If he's serious and he says he is, you're gonna have a tough time putting him off. So if I were you I'd give in gracefully and have my fling. It may not last forever but then, at our time of life, who cares?"

"He said he was serious?"

"Yes."

"But how ...?"

"I asked him. No kidding, Paula. He's hooked. So if you don't want to lose him I'd say it's time to reel him in."

Paula went across to the lift deeply engrossed in what Laura had said, which was why she failed to notice the blue-eyed blond Elmer who was sitting alone by one of the high windows in the hotel lobby.

Elmer's attention had been aroused when Paula came in with Laura Baker and, like a predatory stalker, he had watched her every move until she bade Laura good night and made her way up to her room.

Now he was racing up the back stairs in an effort to reach Paula's door before or at the same time as she did.

Chapter Seven

The evening had proved eventful enough but it was not yet over. Paula was grimly examining her face in the bathroom mirror. Mirrors in hotel bathrooms are notoriously unflattering, she consoled herself. Even here in the glamorous Carlton, the mirror did nothing for her ego. Her figure fared better. Stripped down to her pants and bra she looked trim and neat. A little plump here and there, perhaps. But the curves were still there and, more or less, in the right places.

She was fifty four now, she told herself. All right, fifty five. But all in all she was not so bad. Her short blonde hair was thick and bouncy and, at its best, she knew it could be quite eye-catching. She had good teeth, good skin, good bones and on a good day she could pass for forty. Well, forty five - maybe. She laughed at her harsh reflection in the unfriendly mirror. More like sixty five in this light.

She paused. Someone was tapping at the bedroom door. She listened. It was there again. Wouldn't be Rose. Rose would not be back for ages yet. But there was no mistake, a quiet insistent tap-tap at the door. Paula pulled on her M&S dressing gown.

"Who is it?"

"It's..." A hushed voice. "It's Mr Brodsky's boy, Mrs Blossom."

Paula opened the door slightly.

The blue-eyed blond Elmer, cool and elegant in white slacks, a pale maroon and white-striped Italian shirt and expensive-looking sneakers, gazed down at her like a lost child, the large eyes eager and apologetic.

"What is it?" Paula asked, expecting some message concerning Brodsky, though she couldn't think what.

"I must speak with you, ma'am. It really is important."

Paula hesitated then decided he didn't pose any sort of threat and said, "You'd better come in."

He came in looking excessively grateful, his eyes wide in a way that puzzled Paula. It was Rose who'd had the argument with Brodsky. If he was the bearer of an apology it was Rose he wanted.

"I think you probably want my friend."

"Oh no, Mrs Blossom," he assured her in a kind of hoarse whisper and she realised the doe-like gaze was supposed to express adoration. "It's you I want."

Paula sat on the edge of one of the beds then stood up at once as if she'd received a mild electric shock.

"Er ... sit down," she ordered, a little harshly, and she waved a hand vaguely at a chair by the small round table. He was a lot taller than her and she wanted him cut down to size, a size she could dominate. "What is it, Mr ...?"

"Elmer," he said. "Please call me Elmer, Mrs Blossom."

"So what is it, Elmer?" Paula sat down, facing him on the other upright chair, folded her dressing gown demurely over her knees and held it together at her throat. "What can I do for you?"

The question seemed to strike him like an arrow. Pained, he looked down, shading his eyes theatrically with his hand.

"Elmer?"

"I want to ask you, ma'am, what movies you've made. I know I should probably know, but if you tell me I'll make darned sure I catch them all just as soon as I get back home. I mean, people in the business will think I'm some kind of moron not knowing your movies but I'm only nineteen, ma'am. Eighteen, if I'm honest. An' there's so much I don't know, so much I have to learn." He paused then said softly, "There are things I hope you'll be sorta kind enough to teach me."

Paula shrugged. "There must be some mistake," she told him. "I'm not a film actress. I'm not any kind of actress."

"But you're so beautiful."

Paula looked at him sharply. "Have you been drinking?"

"Oh, no, ma'am. I don't touch alcohol. My mom told me I should never drink alcohol or smoke cigarettes and I should learn to do all the good things in life, like swimming and playing tennis and ... you know." His voice trailed. "The good things."

The subtle change in tone alerted Paula. There was more to this little innocent act, she guessed.

"I should learn to do all the good things properly," he went on, his air of innocence returning. "And what's more I should only learn from the best people."

"Well, I'm sorry to disappoint you, Elmer, but there is nothing, absolutely nothing, I can teach you about films or acting."

"Oh, no. I didn't want you to teach me about the business, ma'am. It isn't that."

"Then what?"

"I would like you to teach me about love."

"Love?" Paula almost laughed aloud.

"Please, ma'am. Hear me out. You are a lovely lady and I can tell, I just know somehow, you are a lovely person, too. Well, my mom told me I should wait, save myself until I find the right lady, a lady who can teach me how to do what a woman really wants from a man. I should leave all these silly young girls alone. Girls my age don't know nothin'. I should put my trust in a real woman, a truly fine older lady. Then maybe, when I've leaned what to do and how to do it really well, I might be a worthy person."

"A worthy person?"

"A person worthy of making love. A person who is able and qualified to make love. For making love, ma'am, is the most beautiful expression of life and living that two people can enjoy on God's earth. My mom told me that, ma'am. And she also told me that most people are downright selfish. They don't know what making love is. They don't know how to make each other truly happy but then that's something you have to learn. I want to be worthy, ma'am, and my mom says only the best kind of lady can show me how."

Paula laughed, a little nervously. She couldn't believe what the boy was saying.

"Please, Mrs Blossom," he said quietly. "Don't laugh at me. I'm young. I don't know nothin'. I ain't ever known a woman in the Biblical sense, if you know what I mean. I have a strong, healthy body. I'm physically fit. I do regular work-outs in the gym. My instructor tells me I'm pretty close to being a perfect specimen. And I have these urges. I want to make love to a lovely lady. But it must be a truly fine lady. I want a beautiful, kind, gentle lady like yourself to teach me how, take me in hand, show me the way."

"Show you the door, you mean," Paula said, not sure whether to laugh in his face or be offended.

"Please, Mrs Blossom, don't turn me down. All I

ask is a simple act of kindness. Take me to your bed. Here and now. And show me how to love you. Just once. That's all I ask."

"Is that all?" she said ironically.

He stood up and Paula noticed he really did have a fine physique. She blushed slightly, anxious not to give the wrong signals. She wanted him out and she was not going to risk him turning nasty. You never know, she thought, self-preservation uppermost in her mind now. He was obviously quite barmy.

"This is all very sudden," she heard herself say. "I mean, I'm going to have to think about it, Elmer. It's not a decision I could take lightly."

"But you do understand? It would cost you so little. No one would ever know. And you would be helping an innocent young person to take a confident step along life's rough highway."

My God! she thought. He really is a nut-case, as Rose would say. "You must give me time," she said implying, as calmly as she could, that he should leave. "I will think about this very carefully and I will let you know."

"When?" he demanded and he sat down again. "I'm sorry to press you like this, but please say when. For if your answer is yes then my whole world will come alight and I will be forever in your debt." He hung his head. "But should you feel you must decline I will simply die of embarrassment at having asked you. And, of course, my disappointment will be so great I may never be able to approach a lady ever again."

If this is an act, thought Paula, he's a rotten actor. But she was not certain that it was. "I'll tell you in the next day or two. I have to think about it."

"We are only here until the end of the week." He was calm now, composed, as if asking what time lunch would be ready.

"Tomorrow then," she said decisively. "By dinner time tomorrow evening."

Elmer went down on one knee, his arms clasped about her legs, his blond head pressed into her crotch. "Dear lady. My dear, dear lady. Thank you. Thank you so much."

Paula tried to pull away but when she looked down she saw that he was crying. Tears streamed down the golden tan of his young cheeks.

"Tomorrow then," she said and she held her breath, her legs closed tight, as he dried his eyes on the folds of her dressing gown. This was ridiculous, ludicrous. A joke, perhaps? Rose's doing? Arlene? Both? Taking a grip on the situation she pulled away, urging him towards the door. "Please," she said sternly. "You must go now."

The doe-like look of adoration had returned. "Until tomorrow, lovely lady," he murmured and he kissed and caressed the back of her hand. "And please. Please, please, please. Let it be yes!"

It was early morning when Rose arrived back and Paula was asleep. At breakfast she fully intended to tell Rose of Elmer's visit and outrageous request, but first she asked her about the previous night. "You were very late back."

"Seven a.m.," Rose confirmed with a smile. "You were well away. You didn't hear a thing."

"You slept with Herbie?"

"Guilty, your honour."

"And was it good?"

"It was fine."

Paula glanced at her sidelong.

"No, really. It was okay," Rose protested. "Not worth sitting through two hours of a French film with sub-titles for, but yeah - it was okay."

Then Herbie and a man they had not previously met joined them and other things happened to claim their attention. Later, as they strolled out on to the terrace for their share of the mid-morning sunshine, they saw Laura Baker and Arlene. Paula and Rose waved and the two waved back. No sign of Tom, Paula noted. Or Marvyn Brodsky or the hopeful Elmer. In response to Rose's question, Herbie said he hadn't seen either Brodsky or the French actor, Phillipe, since the fracas of the night before.

"From what I hear," Herbie's male friend said, with reference to Phillipe, "he's sure as hell blown it."

"With Marvyn, yes," Herbie agreed. "But that makes him okay with almost every other director you can name."

They laughed but what Herbie said was probably true. More than one producer would take Phillipe on board if it meant Marvyn Brodsky would stay away. And more than one actress would, for the same reason, be happy to work with Phillipe.

Herbie and friends, it turned out, had been invited to join a 'hair-of-the-dog' party on a private stretch of beach rented for the duration of the Festival by the exporter of a world famous champagne. Naturally, as the champagne flowed freely at these morning sessions, when it came to invitations there was never any shortage of takers. Freddie, the champagne exporter and not entirely reluctant regular of the gossip columns, was a charming host and so one of the most exclusive stretches of sand anywhere in the world was for a few hours each morning a much coveted venue for invited guests only.

Herbie introduced Paula and Rose to the man he and almost everyone else called Freddie 'Champers'. Freddie took an immediate and obvious liking to Paula.

"You've cracked it here, kiddo," Rose murmured, out of the corner of her mouth. "Free plonk for life."

Paula looked for Tom, but he was nowhere in sight.

"I understand he's working up a deal with the studio," Herbie explained. "But as long as he's free to work for me this winter I don't mind."

"This winter?" Rose queried. "And where will that be?"

"LA, if that's what he wants," Herbie told her. "But he can work wherever he likes until we start shooting. He can write anywhere."

"I've never been to Los Angeles," Rose said. "In fact, I've never been to the United States. There was always talk of going but we never got round to it. My son's been and Paula's been to Disneyland with her daughter and her grandchildren. But I haven't."

"And you never will," Herbie chuckled, "if this young lady has anything to do with it. I reckon she's out to exterminate you, Rose."

Word had gone round that Marvyn Brodsky had kicked Nina not only out of his bed but out of his picture, too. He wanted to have Phillipe black-listed and he had decided, in his usual vindictive way, that he wanted nothing more to do with Phillipe's former girl friend either. Nina partly blamed Rose for upsetting Marvyn and throwing him into a rage. She was out now, a victim of that rage, with no contract and no prospect of a contract. She was looking, she said, for 'that Eengleesh beetch.'

Nina, her face flushed with a simmering lust for revenge and thirty years younger than Rose, had brushed aside the man at the wicket gate whose job it was to keep out undesirables. Every morning that week, Nina had been present at the party and the perplexed old man on the gate, though he sensed Nina was now somehow *persona non grata*, was not sufficiently sure of himself to deny her entry.

Heads turned as Nina appeared in a bright red dress. The champagne sippers stopped sipping. The gossips stopped gossiping. And all the unfocused attention was suddenly focused on the furious Italian girl.

"Herbie Kay, you bastard!" Nina cried. "Eet was you bring that beetch here! Where is she?"

"You have no right to talk to Mr Kay in that way," the tall Edina said, looking down her nose at Nina.

"Where is she?" Nina screamed.

Herbie put out a protective arm but Rose merely smiled and fended him off. "Don't worry about me, Herb. I don't see any problem here."

"There you are! Beetch!"

"Lookin' for me, air-head?" Rose asked mildly and the people nearby backed away as the onlookers at an imminent gunfight tend to do in cowboy pictures.

"Rose!" Paula was alarmed now for her friend who had suddenly looked small and slightly built when confronted by the statuesque young actress.

"I tear you apart," Nina announced.

Rose stood up. "Ready when you are, crummy knickers."

"Wait! Wait, wait!" Herbie Kay stepped between them. "Now what's this all about, Nina?"

Nina towered over him, a good three inches taller than his five-five, even without her stiletto heels. "She lose for me my beeg chance. She make Meester Broad-key no like me."

"If that's true," Rose intervened, "then I'd say I've done you a favour."

"You no do me favour."

"You should've stuck with your boyfriend," Rose told her. "He's worth ten of Brodsky."

"He ees no my boyfriend. No more. He lose for me everytheeng. I want to work for Meester Broad-key." She took an aggressive step closer to Rose. "I would do anytheeng for my career."

"I believe you," Rose said. "I bet your pants have been up an' down like a yo-yo!"

Nina flew at Rose, claws out, but Rose simply stepped aside, caught Nina's hand and swung it up her back. Nina squealed with pain.

"Sorry, my love," Rose said, increasing the pressure slightly, "but you're no match for me. I did Judo last year. Evening classes. Twelve lessons it was and when I'd done I could tie any woman, or any fella for that matter, in a bundle of knots and throw 'em away. I'm down for Car Maintenance next year."

Nina was struggling and squealing but Rose was not even out of breath. "Now if I let you go will you promise to calm down? Behave yourself?"

She struggled more. Rose exerted the necessary pressure and Nina squealed again.

"All right?" Rose asked. "Ready to calm down?"

Gradually, warily, she released the wriggling actress.

But the moment she was free Nina threw herself back into the attack. Yet again Rose caught and twisted her arm and again Nina squealed in pain.

"Ladies! Ladies!" A large, elderly Englishman attempted to mediate. "All this good champagne going begging, it doesn't make sense. Let's bury our differences and simply enjoy."

"I bury you, you beeg fart!" Nina screamed.

"Oh, I say!" the old gentleman exclaimed, his florid features breaking into gales of laughter. "Your command of the English language is most impressive, my dear."

With an apologetic smile, Paula turned to the host. "I do hope we haven't spoiled your party."

But Freddie was enjoying the spectacle. "No, no," he assured her. "Great fun! Really is! Think I'll hire a hall and let them slug it out. What do you say, Herbie old chap?"

"What? Gloves and a ring? Queensberry rules?" Herbie laughed. "I don't know about that. Big as she is, I reckon Nina is no match for my Rosie."

My Rosie, noted Paula. Things must have gone well last night! "Don't you think we should do something?"

Herbie made a face, but again he stepped in to separate them. "Nina, now you listen to me. Marvyn Brodsky is no longer on my next picture. Okay? I have something lined up for later this year. If you're a good girl and you stop all this nonsense, I believe there could be something in it for you."

Nina thought this over.

"Ask him what he means by 'good girl'," Arlene called out with a laugh.

"He means she won't have to climb into bed with anyone," Rose announced sternly.

"Not unless she wants to, of course," Herbie added.

Rose elbowed him hard in the ribs. "Those days are over for you, lover boy."

Paula raised her eyebrows at Rose and wondered exactly what was going on.

"All right?" Herbie asked Nina. "Are you happy with that? A part in my new picture?"

Pouting her lips like a little girl, Nina nodded once.

"Good," Herbie said. "Now shake hands with Rose and let's have no more of this nonsense."

Nina shook her head.

"No picture," Herbie threatened gently.

"But why? Why should I?"

"Shake hands with Rose or there's no part."

Paula turned to Arlene. "Does he mean it?" she whispered. "A part in his picture?"

Arlene nodded. "For now, I guess." Then she shrugged. "Whether he will when he starts casting..."

Reluctantly the Italian girl held out her hand. Rose took it warily. "If I were you," Rose advised her, "I would look out for Phillipe. He obviously thinks a hell of a lot more of you than Brodsky does."

"It's true, Nina," Paula said. "Phillipe put his own career at risk because he didn't like the way Brodsky was treating you."

At that Nina burst into tears and both Paula and Rose moved in to comfort her.

The florid old English gent, it turned out, was a retired Army officer living the life of what used to be called a remittance man. "He was a career soldier," Freddie Champers said in response to a question. "Great fun and a jolly good friend to have. They call him the colonel but, in fact, he was a brigadier. Got cashiered for bumming his batman in Bangalore."

"Come on, Freddie," Tom said, with a laugh. "You're making that up."

"No, really," Freddie insisted. "He'll tell you himself, old chap. Gay as a gargoyle."

Tom had arrived, bearing flutes of champagne, one for Paula and one for himself. And Paula hadn't missed the fleeting suggestion of a frown that furrowed his brow at the word 'gay'.

"Don't you approve of gays then?" she asked quietly.

Tom shrugged. "Nothing against them. Nothing at all. There are lots of them in this business and some of them are my friends."

"Then what?"

"I don't mind homosexuals. What they do in private is up to them. I just object to the way they have appropriated, or perhaps I should say misappropriated, the word 'gay'. It's a lovely word and it's meant to express a certain *joie de vivre* - not a way of life. I say they should give it back and call themselves something else."

"Quite right." The colonel had overheard the tail end of the conversation. His ruddy cheeks aglow, he picked up his glass of champagne and held it high. "In my youth I was carefree and gay. I was also homosexual. Still am, obviously. Difference is, I can say so now. Dare not speak its name in those days, old boy."

"Ah, but then you were called some pretty cruel things, colonel."

"I know, Tom. Poofter, queer, fruit - I've had them all and I must say I'd rather be called gay any day. But I do agree. We've a damned cheek to steal such a lovely word."

"Well, I want it back," Tom told him stubbornly, though with good humour. "I want the word 'gay' returned to its former glory. I want it to mean what it used to mean."

Freddie Champers took up the cause. "The last time I saw Paris," he sang. "My heart was young and gay."

"Sure," Tom said. "And why not? I'd like to be gay again and whenever I feel like it - with the lady of my choice, of course."

"We'll start a campaign for the reclamation of the word," Freddie declared. "Call the Press and Television."

"The Press are partly to blame," someone pointed out. "Short words fit into headlines."

"We must declare war!" Freddie went on undaunted. "Let's tell the world we're feeling gay and we intend to fight for the return of the word to its true meaning."

There was a ripple of applause and a good-natured murmur of approval that turned to laughter when Rose warned, "You better fight with your backs to the wall."

The colonel put an arm around Rose's shoulders. "I do like this little lady of yours, Herbie," he said. "If I were you I wouldn't let her out of my sight. In fact, the sooner you two are married the better."

At the first opportunity Paula took Rose to one side. "What's going on, Rose?" she demanded. "What's all this about you and Herbie and why don't I know about it?"

"Paula, love, I'm sorry. But it came right out of the blue. Herbie asked me to marry him."

"When?"

"Last night."

"But..."

"I know I could have told you first thing but I wanted to think about it. I mean, he might have changed his mind this morning. He hasn't, as it happens. He asked me again at breakfast."

"The colonel knew..."

Rose nodded. "Herbie must have discussed it with him. I know he shouldn't have and I don't know how many others he's told. But I'm sorry. I wanted to wait until we were alone and we could talk it over. Just the two of us. Together."

"Do you want to marry him?"

Rose nodded and laughed nervously. "I know it sounds crazy but yes, I do. I just love the fat dope."

"Well," Paula said, with a shrug, "if you're sure there's nothing more to talk about."

"Paula! Don't be like that."

"I'm not being like anything," Paula said. "If you want to marry him and you're sure, then why not? There's nothing to stop you. It doesn't concern anyone else, except perhaps your Phil. What would he say?"

"I don't know. There's no reason why he should object. I should think he'd be glad of someone to take me off his hands."

"Oh no!" Paula was quick to defend Rose's ever smiling son. "He's not like that. Not Phil."

"Knowing Phil," Rose said, with a laugh, "he'll probably want Herbie to get him a job in pictures."

Herbie came alongside and for once he looked sheepish and anxious for approval. "What do you think, Paula?"

"I think it's lovely, Herbie. I really do. I was a bit stunned at first but then I thought - why not?" Paula kissed him lightly on the cheek. "I wish you all the luck in the world and I hope you'll both be very happy."

He was clearly delighted with her response. "I thought end of next week, before we go West, I'd take Rosie home to meet my old lady."

"And where is home, Herbie?" Paula asked.

He smiled. "Stepney."

Tom had been cornered by the colonel and two of the colonel's flamboyant friends.

"Hang on," Herbie said. "This calls for a celebration lunch. I'll just go and rescue Tom."

Rose and Paula watched him go and Paula laughed as if totally bewildered. "I'm amazed," she said. "I can't keep up with all this."

"Well, if you've any sense, Paula Blossom," Rose told her, "you'll grab Tom while you can."

Arlene, who'd had rather more than her share of the morning's champagne, came across nodding in agreement. "She's right, Paula, absolutely right. Better grab him quick before the party's over."

Chapter Eight

They'd had lunch on a quayside terrace, just the four of them. Now, outside the restaurant, under an awning of green and white stripes, it was pleasant to sit back with a pot of steaming coffee, Herbie and Tom with their drams of cognac, and watch the passing crowd. Separated from the cobbled expanse of the quay by a low wall topped with wooden containers from which grew spring flowers of pink and pale blue, they were happily marginalised with no inclination to move on.

Tourists and merchant seamen mingled with delivery boys and tradesmen. Out on the quay at an improvised stall an old woman in the black garb of a Mediterranean matriarch sold cheap mementoes. And the sun shone on the wide variety of sea-going vessels, some sparkling white, some peeling with patches of rust and in need of paint, others in the process of renovation.

Rose and Herbie, with their newly announced togetherness, had scraped their chairs close until they and their chairs were almost touching. Tom was sitting, as he always did when accompanied by a lady, with his back to the passing scene, thus ensuring that his companion had the best of the view. In Paula's book this was one of the hallmarks of a true gentleman. Today, however, though Tom had not abandoned his usual gallantry, a little chasm appeared to have opened up between them, as if they were unconnected guests at the celebration.

"Got to watch my figure now," Rose declared. "Got to get in trim for the wedding."

Herbie lifted her hand and kissed it. "No problem,

sweetheart. I like you just the way you are."

"Oh, you do, do you?" she said, her eyebrows raised. "Well, you can just get yourself into shape, too. I'm not marrying any roly-poly."

"I'm the one who'll have to watch my weight," Paula said ruefully. "I put on pounds if I'm not careful."

"You're my bridesmaid," Rose told her.

"And Tom's my best man," Herbie added.

"And when is this wedding?" Tom asked. "And where?"

"Has to be LA," Herbie said, glancing at Rose.

Rose shrugged. "Fine by me. And Paula's no excuse." She faced Paula. "So don't say you have."

"Los Angeles?" Paula said. "When?"

"Before we start shooting, I reckon," Herbie said, turning the logistics over in his mind. "September, maybe." He looked at all three in turn. "That okay?

A gypsy girl selling sprigs of violets pushed a bunch under his nose. Normally Herbie would have waved the girl away but he paid her ungrudingly and handed the flowers to Rose. Tom made no attempt to do the same for Paula and the gypsy girl moved on.

"Some time in September in LA," Herbie continued.

"And what do we do until then?" Rose asked. "Paula and I are due home this week-end."

"We go up North to see your son then we go see my old mother. Then, kid, we fly off into the blue. You can stay in my guest house until we're well and truly wed."

"I'll think about it," Rose said. "You know I don't hold with this living over the brush."

"You wouldn't be living over the brush," Herbie assured her. "It's completely separate. Ask Tom. He's stayed there often enough."

"How big is it?"

"Two bedrooms, bathroom, kitchen, living room - plenty big enough."

Paula felt that she and Tom were intruders, listening in to a private conversation.

"Paula could stay with me," Rose said.

"Sure," Herbie agreed at once. "Why not?"

"I don't know what you're worried about," Paula told her. "Everybody lives over the brush nowadays."

"Well, I'm not everybody," Rose said.

"You'd like it, Paula," Tom said, addressing her dispassionately. "It's plenty big enough for two."

Rose had not missed the subtle distancing of Tom and Paula. "And what's next for you, Tom?" she asked.

"Well," he said, "I've got a writing job before the big day, but I'll be back home for the wedding."

"Are you staying in Europe then?" Paula asked.

"I'm not sure. Steve Hogan wants me to do a screenplay for him. It's a good story and I'm looking forward to doing it."

"You got to get it done," Herbie warned him. "No overlapping, okay?"

"I'll be ready when you want me," Tom assured him with a smile. "September in LA. I'll make a note."

Paula was finding the pace of events just a little too rapid. But Rose was taking everything in her stride. Already she had one foot firmly placed in this new world and appeared to have no qualms about leaving the old.

The signs had been there, Paula realised, but she had missed them. Take the smoking. At home, even after appealing in nightly prayers to the Almighty, Rose had failed to give it up. Now, to Paula's delight, she claimed to have succeeded. To be fair, in deference to Paula's good-natured but firm strictures on the perils of passive smoking, Rose had taken to having her pre-breakfast cigarette out on the balcony. These last two or three mornings she had foregone even this indulgence.

"I have to give it up," Rose had announced. "Herbie doesn't like to see girls smoking."

"What about him and his cigars?" Paula had laughed.

Rose had simply shrugged. "He hardly ever lights them."

Paula recalled, too, how swiftly Rose came to Herbie's defence whenever she felt it necessary. Once an ageing and apparently bitter actress had made totally unwarranted and derogatory remarks about Herbie's physical stature. "Why," she had proclaimed loudly and in the grand manner she had once employed on the so-called silver screen, "that little bantam can't be more than five-four."

Edina, surprisingly, had been quick to respond with, "Only a whore measures a man's worth in inches." And Rose had applauded with overstated and enthusiastic approbation, informing all present, "Hey! I wish I'd said that!"

There was a possessiveness, too, a hint of jealousy that was surprising in Rose, another clue that Paula realised now she ought to have spotted. It was most marked on one occasion when Herbie had expressed a passing interest in an up-and-coming young French actress. Don't you think she has a look of Ginger Rogers? he had asked innocently. Rose could not have been more scathing. Nah! she said. She looks more like Fred Astaire.

So Rose had got her man and Paula hadn't even

realised it was happening. You have been too engrossed in your own affairs, she told herself, and especially this affair with Tom, if that's what it is.

"What is it with you and Tom?" Rose asked later.

Back in their room at the Carlton, Paula sat on the bed, puzzled and more than a little disconcerted. "I don't know," she admitted airily. "But whatever it is it's none of my doing."

"You've had a falling out?"

"Not that I know of."

"Then what is it?"

"I don't know, Rose. I expect he's gone off me, that's all. It happens. Happens all the time."

"All right. Don't get upset."

"I'm not upset."

"You could have fooled me."

"Go and have your shower," Paula said and she went to the dressing table, sat down and looked at the photograph of her husband Ted.

She thought of the letter Ted had left for her, the letter in which he had urged her to do something for herself, take a holiday, anything. There were parts of that letter that were strictly private, parts that she would never want to show to anyone else, and she recalled those parts now, every word.

One thing he had told her, though not in an unkind way, was that she should allow herself to experience physical love. 'A man can't make love to a woman who won't let him touch her,' he had written. She had been squeamish, it was true. She didn't like him to touch her breasts or do anything other than accept his marital rights in the most straightforward manner. But Ted had been too much of a gentleman and too much in control to persist and eventually their love-making, such as it was, had simply lapsed. It had become something they used to do, like play tennis.

Once, when she had confided in Rose that Ted didn't bother any more, Rose had asked with her usual delicacy, You sure he isn't getting it somewhere else? Paula had laughed and replied with total confidence that she always knew where he was and who he was with. And this was true. Most of the time Ted was away from home he was in his office with the occasional day or two at a conference of some kind or other, nothing on a regular basis where illicit contacts could be made and maintained and she was certain he was not one for casual encounters.

"He had a secretary who was in love with him for twenty years," Paula had told Rose. "But she was fifteen years older than him, an old-fashioned spinster."

"There you are then," Rose had countered, as if Paula had justified her suspicion.

But Paula had laughed again. "She hated men. The only two men she could bring herself to speak to were Ted and the vicar at the Parish Church."

"Like I said, there you are then. You can bet one of 'em was getting his leg over."

"You would only have to see her," Paula had replied with a smile, "to know that's not true."

But Rose had refused to recant. "Don't you believe it. They have hidden depths some of these old spinsters."

Paula had laughed even louder. Rose could be surprisingly silly at times. Ted's former secretary was a nice, if strait-laced lady, precise and good at her job, her friend as well as Ted's. She was more like a maiden aunt than an employee and Rose was way off the mark.

What concerned Paula now, more than anything, was the way she, herself, had denied Ted. He had tried for a time to initiate something, to rekindle what they once had. Although that last phrase was not strictly accurate. There had been nothing much to rekindle. At least, not on a physical level. They had performed the exercises necessary to produce two children but they had rarely made love for its own sake. Or, to be precise, Paula hadn't.

When he was younger, Ted, like most healthy young men, must have found the release a necessity. But, Paula realised now, the perfunctory procedure they went through must have been far from satisfactory. Satisfying, perhaps, for an instant - for Ted. But never deeply so and never at all for her. And it was her fault. She knew that then and she knew it now and she was sorry.

She had loved him and she loved the memory of him and all they had meant to each other and she longed for another chance to make it work. She believed she could do it now and she longed just for the chance, the chance to open up like a flower in the sun, slowly and sensuously, with total commitment and without restraint.

Once, on holiday in Madeira, they had met a French couple. Ted had got into conversation with the Frenchman because he, Ted, considered himself 'good at French'. A doctor of medicine, the Frenchman was a general practitioner in a suburb of Paris. He was a charming, worldly, silver-haired man who spoke English with an accent that seemed to caress the words and was a joy to hear.

His wife was tall, slim and quite beautiful despite the loss of her hair and eyebrows to several courses of chemotherapy. She wore a little black hat or, rather, headband which she never removed in public. But she spoke openly of the cancer in her lungs. Retired in her mid-fifties, she had once been European Sales Director for an international cigarette company and, as a consequence, in the course of her work, she had smoked the company's products to excess. Now she was paying the price.

What Paula especially remembered about that French couple was the way in which they spoke to each other, the way their eyes met from time to time, the way they touched hands, their unobtrusive closeness. The lady's name was Janine, but her husband invariably called her 'Janni'. Watching them Paula had realised how close, how intimate her life with Ted could be. But even then she had failed to do anything about it.

This was why it had hurt so much when Ted's posthumous letter had urged her to live, to enjoy what was left of her life, to embrace whatever new experiences came her way and - the lines that struck home hardest of all - if someone new comes along try to be open and accessible, and if he truly loves you try hard to love him in return.

It wasn't fair, she told herself. She had always assumed there would be time, time for them to talk, time for her to make clear to Ted how she felt about him, how much she really loved him. But he had been taken from her and the letter he had left - though this had not been his intention - made her cry whenever she read it.

Thankfully, thought Paula, Rose is still in the bathroom. She didn't want to have to explain or hide the tears in her eyes. But she felt she must talk to Rose and with some urgency, find out how and why Rose had agreed to marry Herbie Kay and exactly what her friend was getting into. Things seemed to be happening just a little too fast for Paula's liking.

Rose came out of the bathroom, a towel coiled about her head, the complimentary white bathrobe clutched to her chest.

"So what's going on, Rose? What on earth is going on?" Paula laughed, a bright puzzled laugh. "All this is beyond me. My cleaner is going off with a movie mogul. You're a cleaning lady, for goodness sake! What about your job?"

"Sod that for a start!" Rose danced around the bedroom in the large bulky robe as if to a waltz. "Cinderella is going to marry the prince."

"Well," Paula began, "he may not be the most handsome prince in the world..."

"I don't care what he looks like," Rose cut in with a laugh. "And who knows? With any luck, if I kiss him often enough, he might turn into a frog."

"I was about to say, Herbie is a very nice fellow. I like him very much and I hope you'll be very happy together. But I fail to see why you have to marry him."

Rose stopped waltzing. "I don't have to marry him. I mean, I'm not pregnant!"

"I know you're not pregnant," Paula said. "I don't believe in miracles any more than you do. What I want to know is why you have to marry him."

"You know why," Rose said. "I don't hold with this living over the brush."

"People don't worry about that sort of thing any more. Most youngsters wouldn't dream of getting married nowadays without having a trial run."

"I know. But we're not youngsters, are we, Paula? And our generation - well, I know some do it - but I don't approve. And I don't believe you do, either. I mean, would you live with Tom if you were not married?"

"He hasn't asked me," Paula said.

"But if he did?"

"I don't know," Paula said and then, dismissively, "and it's not likely to happen, is it?"

"Not if you insist on treating him the way you do."

"And what way is that?"

"Cool," Rose said. "Off-hand. The poor man needs some encouragement."

"We were talking about you and Herbie. Now let's be honest, Rose. Do you love Herbie, a man you barely know? Or is it what he has to offer?"

"Does it matter?" Rose smiled and began to uncoil the towel from about her head. "This last week or so, this holiday, Paula, it's been the greatest thing that ever happened to me. I've never had such a good time. I love it and I want it to go on forever - and maybe, if I marry Herbie, it will."

That evening Paula and Rose found they were to dine alone. Herbie was to attend a private meeting with the sheik in Nice and Tom had a script conference followed by dinner with the Hogan family, for some reason at the Hotel Gray d'Albion just behind the Croisette.

"Left to our own devices," Paula commented.

"Vices, you mean," Rose said and she suggested they should host a ladies evening with Laura Baker and Arlene as their guests.

"Better ask Edina, too," Paula said.

Rose made a face. "I'll make sure Arlene and Laura can come first. I mean, we wouldn't want to be stuck with just Edina, would we now?"

Laura said she would be delighted. Arlene said she had a dinner date but not one she couldn't cancel. And even Edina said yes. Her husband, Jim, had been moaning on all day, she said, about having an early night. Well, he could have one. She would tuck him up in bed and be down for eight thirty, if that was all right.

The waiter in the cocktail bar could not have been more attentive and the five girls teased him relentlessly about his love life. Rose announced that in celebration of her engagement to Herb - though she didn't have a ring to show for it yet - dinner was on her.

"Sting him good, babe," Arlene advised. "He's got pots of money stashed away."

"You don't know that," Laura said.

"Come on, Laura," Arlene insisted. "Movie makers like Herb only spend other people's money."

"That's what Jim used to do," Edina agreed, looking far more relaxed without her cantankerous husband. "But he isn't rich. He saved it and I spent it."

They laughed appreciatively and as Paula turned her head she saw Elmer, Brodsky's boy, who was hovering by the door. He smiled at her as if besotted and she nodded coolly before turning back to her companions, hoping none of them had noticed.

Arlene, who missed very little, leered knowingly. "Who's been playing Elmer's tune then?"

Paula decided there was no reason why she shouldn't confide in her friends, see what they made of Elmer's outrageous advances, but just then a tall slim Frenchman stopped by their table on his way to the bar.

He had a thin, neat moustache, dyed black now like his slick-backed hair, and Paula thought of the old-style film heart-throbs, men like Gilbert Roland and Caesar Romero.

"Arlene, ma dahleen," he gushed. "How are you, ma sweetheart?"

Arlene smiled sweetly. "Same as I was when you asked me at lunch time."

"You introduce me to these lovely ladies?"

"Not until you learn to behave yourself."

He took the red rose from his lapel and laid it on the table before her. "I will try again tomorrow and the next day and the next day until I am forgiven." He bowed low and acknowledged the others with a flourish and his most debonair smile. "*Mesdames*!"

As he withdrew gracefully the others craned forward, eager for Arlene to elaborate.

"Go on then, tell us," Paula urged. "What did he do?"

"I socked him one," Arlene answered evasively, but this only fuelled their curiosity.

"What did he *do*?" Rose demanded.

"Is he an actor or something?" Paula asked.

No, Arlene explained, he was not an actor. Not professionally, anyway. He was a sort of French playboy.

Laura Baker knew the man well. "The personification of Gallic charm," she laughed, "at least, according to his press agent."

"More like phallic charm if you ask me," Edina put in unexpectedly and they all laughed, warming again to her dry humour. The old girl, it seemed to Paula and Rose, could be quite a wit.

The Frenchman's name was René and he was a flyer. A licensed pilot. He owned a small aeroplane, Arlene went on, a Cessna or a Cherokee or something like that, and the other morning he had offered to take her for a spin. She laughed. " 'Come fly with me, come let us fly away,' he said, 'and once we're up there, I'll let you hold my joystick!' So I socked him one."

The others erupted and the hilarity that followed encouraged Paula to tell them about the boy, Elmer. He had come to her room late at night, she told them, and she had been foolish enough to let him in. She thought he had some message for Rose. From Brodsky. An apology or something. But he said he hadn't. He said it was her, Paula, he wanted.

Again the group round the table craned forward as in a scrum down.

"He said he wanted to know what movies I'd made and then he said there was so much for him to learn. He wanted me to teach him." Paula laughed. "I told him he was mistaken. I'm not an actress, never have been, but he said he didn't mean acting. He wanted me to teach him about the good things in life."

"Hold on," Rose cut in. "And where was I when all this was going on?"

"In bed with Herbie, if you remember."

Rose nodded. "So go on."

"He wanted me to teach him how to make love."

"He what?" Rose looked at her in disbelief.

"Honestly. That's what he said."

Arlene and Laura looked at each other knowingly.

"His mom!" Arlene said.

"His mom told him to save himself," Laura went on, "find the right lady." She laughed. "He's not to drink or smoke cigarettes and he's to keep himself fit and healthy and ready to learn from some respectable old broad who really knows what a woman wants from a man."

"But how?" Paula began, then it dawned on her that Elmer had tried it on with both Arlene and Laura and she laughed in embarrassment. "Of all the cheek!"

"Come on," Rose pressed her. "What happened? This young fella comes to our room late at night and asks you to teach him how to make love. *You*?"

"Yes. *Me*!" Paula responded haughtily. "Why shouldn't he ask me?"

"Well, why didn't he ask me?"

"All right, you two," Laura said, laughing. "I'm sure you won't have to fight over him. He'll let you both teach him, if you ask."

"And at the same time, too, I shouldn't wonder," Arlene added.

"Well, getting rid of him wasn't easy. He gave me a lecture on how, according to his mom, making love is the most beautiful experience of life and living on God's earth - or something like that. He wanted me to share it with him, teach him how to do it right. I had to promise I'd think about it."

"Oh, yeah?" Laura said. "I told him I'd kick his ass half-way up the Croisette."

"The cheeky young sod!" Rose said.

Arlene laughed. "I told him I didn't interfere with minors and he should come back in about ten years time." She shrugged defensively. "I mean, I might be glad of a young Adonis by then."

They looked at Edina who wore an enigmatic smile on her usually austere countenance.

"You don't mean...?" Arlene began.

Edina shook her head. "I'm saying nothing."

They all laughed again and Rose said, "Now let me get this straight. He makes a habit of this. He asks older women to jump into bed with him under the pretext that it's all new to him, he's never done it before and he wants a few lessons."

"Apparently, yes," Paula said.

"And sometimes he gets lucky?" she queried.

"Sure to," Laura said. "Law of averages."

"You can bet on it," Arlene said. "I reckon there are plenty of notches on his pina colada."

"Well," Paula said, laughing nervously, "I don't want to be a notch on his penis, thank you very much."

"Oh, I don't know," Rose said, for a laugh. "He's a good-looking lad. He can carve my name on his Roll of Honour any time."

"In that case," Paula told her, "you can give him his lessons."

"Speaking of which," Arlene said thoughtfully, "I reckon it's time we all taught him a little lesson."

Laura laughed. "We could do a Mrs Bobbit."

"Oh no!" Edina said, with a shudder. "Nothing so drastic, I hope."

"No, no." Arlene agreed. "Just something that, for the rest of his life, whenever he thinks about it, will send an almighty chill up his ass!"

Chapter Nine

The lady was willing and Elmer couldn't believe his luck. The little page boy had handed him a note in the lobby of the hotel only minutes after his boss, Marvyn Brodsky, had given him the evening off. 'My friend, Mrs Parker, will be away for the night and I shall have the room to myself,' the note read. 'So tonight's the night! Come up to 404 at 11.30 for lesson number one - Mrs B.'

A rather pretty girl, whom Elmer had bedded twice in the past few nights, asked him when he was going to introduce her to his boss. Preoccupied with the note from Paula, he looked at her as if he didn't know her, turned on his heel and left her near to tears as she fended off the overtures of a lecherous old drunk.

Way out at sea the lights of a cruise ship grew gradually smaller. Elmer gazed up at the bright glitter of stars in the black velvet sky, his eyes shining as he rubbed his crotch in eager anticipation. Oh, what a night this was going to be! Lesson number one, she had written. Did that mean there would be more?

Later in the dining room he saw Mrs Blossom at a table with four other ladies and later still he saw the old producer's wife leave to go back to her husband. Elmer decided to lie low, keep out of the way. He didn't want to embarrass Mrs B in front of her friends and he certainly didn't want to run any risk of her changing her mind.

Hair combed, teeth brushed, like a small boy on his first day at school, Elmer presented himself at the door of room 404 at precisely 11.30.

"Come in!" a voice answered in response to his discreet little knock. Carefully he opened the door and looked inside. Mrs Blossom was sitting at the dressing table, combing her hair.

"Mrs Blossom," he said, coming in and closing the door behind him.

She turned to greet him with a bright smile, the comb held high. "Paula. You may call me Paula."

"When I got your note ..." he began.

Paula held up her hands to keep him, for the moment, at bay. "Wait! Elmer, you must do exactly as I say."

"Of course," he breathed. "Whatever..."

"I want you to know," Paula said sternly, "I have never done this sort of thing before."

"Nor have I, dear lady?" Elmer lied.

"What I want to say is, we must take our time. We have all night. So there is no hurry."

"Of course," Elmer said again, eager to please.

"Well then," Paula said, standing up.

His cheeks were pink with anticipation. Paula suddenly felt sorry for him. She was beginning to regret having agreed to do what she was doing but she had come this far, the lad was here and there was no backing out.

At the wall she switched on the bedside lamps and switched off the chandelier. "I want you to undress, take off all your clothes, everything, and put them on this chair - neatly." She realised she must sound like some kind of medic or, worse still, his mother. She smiled and tried to soften her voice. "Will you do that for me?"

Now, she felt, she sounded like a nanny addressing her infant charge. Obediently Elmer pulled his shirt out of his pants and began to unfasten the buttons.

"Take your time, dear," Paula said. "I shall go into the bathroom and make myself ready. There's no hurry."

Elmer thought otherwise. He already had the biggest erection he'd had in weeks and he wanted to be free of his clothing. He pulled off his trainers and his tennis socks. Then he pulled off his jeans and his polka dot, designer underpants.

He looked round the room, cupped the throbbing penis in his fist. God! he hoped it wasn't going to let him down! He wanted it to stay like this, as stiff and as hard as a gendarme's truncheon. Hopping on one foot, he wished she'd hurry up. He couldn't wait for the 'lesson' to begin.

There was something about Mrs Blossom, something special. She may not be conventionally beautiful and as physically perfect as Arlene and the other movie madams but she was totally feminine, all woman. She was also more refined than most and he'd been more than merely surprised when she'd agreed. But you could never tell who was going to take you up at this game. Which was why it paid to try them all.

The bathroom door opened slightly and Paula stuck a bare leg out. Elmer's mouth fell open. Then, in high heeled shoes and wrapped, or so it seemed, in only her dressing gown, Paula emerged.

"My!" she exclaimed, noting his fist. "You *are* glad to see me."

"Paula," he said softly, moving towards her.

Paula held up her hands. "I'm the teacher. And you must do exactly as I say."

He nodded, beginning to be embarrassed by his still enormous erection.

"I want you to lie on the bed," she told him. "I want you to lie face down."

"Face down?"

"To begin with, yes," she said briskly. "Go on."

A little puzzled, Elmer lay face down on the nearest of the twin beds.

"Now put you hands behind your back," she ordered. "Come on. I want us to try this first. I promise you, this is something you have never experienced before."

You can say that again, thought Elmer, and it crossed his mind that she might be mad, some kind of nut. But he did as he was told, reassured as she sat astride him on the bed, though he realised now she was not entirely naked under her dressing gown.

"Hands behind your back," she ordered and she took a large roll of sellotape from her patch pocket. "Hold still."

"What...?"

"It's all right," she said soothingly and she began to bind his wrists with the tape. "This is something new. I promise."

"What is it, Paula? What are you ...?"

"It's all right, my darling," she told him softly. "Just relax."

Round and round and up and over she bound the tape.

"There now. It has to be completely secure. You must not be able to escape."

"I'd have to be Harry Houdini."

"All right then. That's fine." Paula stepped away from the bed. "You can get up now."

Elmer stood up, his hands tied tightly behind his back,

his penis, surprisingly, still erect.

"You can come out now, girls," Paula called out and Laura, Arlene and Rose fell in from the bathroom.

"Wow!" Rose cried. "What a whopper!"

"What a waste," Arlene murmured in admiration.

Elmer tried to laugh the situation off. "Come on now, ladies. It was just a joke."

"I guess the joke's on you, kid," Laura laughed.

Arlene and Rose were each wielding a long, prickly stem from the bouquet the sheik Bondi had sent.

"Very prickly these roses, absolutely lethal," Arlene threatened and she made a practice lunge. Then they advanced, stems outstretched, and he was forced to retreat until his back was to the wall.

"Okay," he said, worried now. "You win and I'm sorry."

Rose went to the dressing table drawer and drew out a large pair of scissors.

"Hey now!" Elmer cried in alarm. "A joke's a joke."

"This is no joke, sonny," Arlene said, her face set like a threat, and she took the scissors.

Elmer's erection had begun to wilt. Beads of perspiration had appeared on his golden brow. He swallowed hard. But the only thing Arlene cut was the wide band of pale blue ribbon from the bouquet of flowers.

She handed the scissors back to Rose. "One false move," she said, "and you let him have it."

Kneeling before him on one knee Arlene looped the ribbon under the now drooping penis and, with some aplomb, tied a large decorative bow. "There we go," she said, well satisfied with her work. "First prize for cheek and downright impertinence!"

Elmer felt ridiculous. He had got over the fact that he was in the nude in the presence of four women, each one old enough to be his mother. His ego told him he had a fine body and nothing to be ashamed of, but there was no escape. Paula had done a good job with the sellotape and his wrists were well and truly bound. He was at their mercy.

"Okay," he conceded yet again. "Like I said, you win. I asked for what I got and I don't blame you one bit. So can I go now - please?"

"We finished with him, ladies?" Laura asked.

The others nodded.

Arlene went to the door and swung it open. "Okay. You can go."

"What about my clothes?"

"We'll send them down, won't we, Rose?"

"Right away," Rose said and she gathered up his shirt and the rest of his neatly folded clothing, went to the balcony and threw them out into the night.

"You can't do that," Elmer protested.

"I just did," Rose told him, with a smile.

"And I can do this," Arlene said and she picked up his trainers and socks and threw them out, too.

Elmer looked horrified. "But..."

"Goodbye, Elmer," they chorused and Rose held the scissors aloft.

"I can't go out. Not like this."

He glanced at the bed as if he might snatch a sheet but they advanced on him, waving their prickly thorns. With the scissors Rose made as if to snip at his not so private parts and he withdrew at once, back to the wall.

"Come on, girls." he begged, crouching forward and knock-kneed now.

"Out!" Arlene insisted, then the others joined in and it became a chant - "Out! Out! Out!" - as they forced him out into the empty corridor and slammed the door.

The corridor was deserted, an empty street of closed doors. There was nowhere, not even a curtained window, where Elmer could hide. About half-way down on the right, by the lift, there was an automatic shoe polisher and a few brightly lit advertising panels adorned the wall. But there was nothing he could use to cover his confusion.

The indicator arrows were lit and he could hear the whirr of the approaching lift. He ran to the bend of the corridor. More closed doors. The only variation was the double swing doors to the stairs. Elmer stepped through but the landing and the stairway were even less inviting and the uncarpeted floor was cold to his bare feet. He shivered then dodged back as a head and shoulders went by the window squares in the swing doors.

It was a red-faced, well-built man in his mid-forties and he was carrying a pair of black Oxfords. Elmer saw the door to the man's bedroom was slightly ajar. He stepped back into the corridor, tiptoed to the bend and peering round cautiously, saw that the man was at the automatic shoe polisher.

Elmer made a dash for the partly open door, intent on taking a sheet, anything, to cover himself, though just how he would do this with his hands so securely tied behind his back was a problem in itself. Once inside the room he soon realised he had run into more trouble. Oh, my God! he murmured. There was someone in the bathroom.

He heard the red-faced man returning. He cast around for somewhere to hide. The bed was down to within an inch of the floor and there was no way he could crawl beneath it. The wardrobe! It was his only possible refuge. With his little finger he managed to prise open the white door and shoulder his way inside. Moments later the man entered the bedroom.

Ernest and Myrtle Fiedler were 'second time arounders'. They had been married two weeks before in their home town near Columbus, Ohio, and this holiday - in Cannes, France, at the height of the Film Festival - had been Ernie's honeymoon surprise for Myrtle, a dedicated film buff. It had taken some fixing and Ernie was deeply indebted to a former boyfriend of his mother who had somehow succeeded in securing the almost impossible to get room. Ernie was a high blood pressure man likely to blow his top at the slightest slight but also given to surprising enthusiasms about the most inconsequential of matters. Right now, having tested the automatic shoe polisher, he was like a kid with a new toy.

"Shines your shoes real good," Elmer heard him say.

In among the suits and dresses Elmer held his breath. This is crazy, he thought. The guy will go bananas! He tried to move back behind the racks of clothing but the wardrobe was only shallow. Patience, he told himself. Maybe he could stay where he was. It must be midnight by now. With any luck these people would go to bed. Maybe he could wait until they were sound asleep then let himself out. Maybe he could free his hands and find something to wear. His eyes switched from side to side in the near dark. Maybe a pair of the guy's pants would fit.

"You comin' to bed, hon?" the man asked plaintively. "Time's a wasting. There's things we could be doin'."

Oh God! thought Elmer. What if they start screwing?

But then the worst happened and the man came to the wardrobe. "If you ain't ready I guess I'll polish up my ..." He flung open the door as he spoke and took a startled step back. He looked at Elmer in astonishment, at the blue ribbon still tied jauntily to Elmer's penis and a mounting rage suffused his red face to an even darker hue as the situation, as he saw it, slowly dawned on him.

Elmer attempted a conciliatory grin. "I can explain."

"Myrtle!" Ernie exploded. "Get your ass in here!"

"Sir." Elmer was terrified. "It's not what you think."

"Ernie?" Wearing only a flimsy nightdress, Myrtle appeared at the bathroom door. "What is it, dear?"

"What is it?" Ernie cried, as if in pain. "You tell me! This is our honeymoon for Chrissake an' already you got some naked asshole in the goddam wardrobe!"

Elmer dived under the man's arm and dashed for the door. Myrtle screamed and Ernie took up the chase. Down the corridor two couples were just leaving the lift. Elmer raced towards them and squeezed through the closing doors, evading Ernie's outstretched grasp by inches.

"*Mon Dieu*!" one of the men exclaimed.

"Ya see that?" Ernie demanded. "Naked! Not a stitch on!" He frowned. The guy's hands had been tied behind his back and he looked as though he'd won some kind of prize. It was too much for Ernie and he could only gaze at the two couples in wonder. "Kinky bastard, too."

Elmer sank back against the lift door then stuck his

finger in the slot for the second floor. Brodsky's room was on the second floor. Elmer knew he would have some hard explaining to do. He was already in his boss's bad books. But it was his only option. He prayed that no one would be there when the lift door went back and that Brodsky would be in.

The lift jerked gently to a halt and as the door slid open Elmer held his breath. There was no one there. He looked out to the right and to the left, then made a dash for Brodsky's room.

Knocking on the door with his hands tied behind his back was not easy. First he tried with an elbow, then with a knee. There was no response. Brodsky was probably still downstairs, he decided, no doubt lording it over his various underlings in his usual obnoxious manner. He turned and tried with his heel but that was even less effective. Again he tried with an elbow.

Someone called the lift and the whirr began again. He would have to find some place to hide and some way to release his hands. He had strained at the tape and rubbed his wrists together until they hurt and the sheer frustration had brought tears to his eyes. Again he turned and heeled the door, this time in anger.

Come on, you fat slob! he murmured and he thought he heard a movement inside the room. He heeled the door yet again. Maybe he'd managed to raise the great whale of a jerk after all. Come on! Come on!

Getting on the wrong side of Marvyn Brodsky was something Elmer could not afford to risk right now. He tried to compose his face, return it to its accustomed servility, as the door opened slightly and Brodsky peered through the crack. Astounded by what he saw he pulled the door wide open and stared, slack-mouthed at Elmer.

Elmer tried to turn his lower half away from Brodsky's disapproving eyes and indicate that his hands had been tied behind his back. He saw that Brodsky was barefoot and wearing only pyjama bottoms, his disgusting flab revealed in all its corpulent grandeur.

It would be difficult to imagine a less attractive sight, thought Elmer. But he smiled hopefully at his boss, aware that Brodsky would be less than pleased at having been brought from his bed to come to the aid of so lowly a subordinate.

"What in God's name...?"

"Mr Brodsky, sir, I need your help."

Brodsky looked down disdainfully at the blue ribbon. "You sure as hell need somebody's help, you dirty little pervert."

Elmer was suddenly aware of two very young girls, both naked, who were kneeling up on Brodsky's bed and trying to get a better view of him over Brodsky's shoulder. "Mr Brodsky, sir, I can explain."

The girls were ogling Elmer openly now and they ran to the door, squealing hilariously and giggling at his predicament. Brodsky, who may well have been suddenly conscious of and piqued by the unavoidable comparison the girls would make between his own obese wreck of a body and young Elmer's admittedly fine physique, turned characteristically nasty. He pushed Elmer back from the threshold.

"You're fired, you dirty bastard! Go on, beat it. Get out o' my life."

Elmer saw there was no reasoning with the man. He looked back then ran for the bend in the corridor.

"Pervert!" Brodsky called after him.

As he turned the corner Elmer found he was in more trouble. Three elderly ladies in black evening gowns were blocking his progress. They were dripping with the class of jewellery it can take a lifetime to acquire but nothing they were wearing seemed half so exotic as Elmer's blue bow.

One of the ladies, a genteel Englishwoman, had lived at the Carlton for many years and was to swear later, brandishing her *lorgnette*, that in all that time she had never before seen such a sight. Her two friends, dinner guests for the evening, had thoroughly enjoyed the spectacle and for months to come would rib her that her true reason for living permanently at the sumptuous hotel was that Greek god-like young men, gaily festooned and in bondage no less, raced naked round the corridors at midnight.

Elmer had dived for the stairs and stayed there until the elderly ladies had gone by, but when he emerged he was confronted by a lively group of revellers led by the cashiered colonel. The colonel was enchanted by the vision before him and at once began to thank his cohorts. What a beautiful young man! he raved. And what a lovely birthday present! It was not his birthday, he freely admitted. But if this superb boy was up for grabs he would be more than happy to bring it forward. The others cheered, shattering the calm of the quiet corridor, and assured him Elmer was for him. Again Elmer dived for the stairway.

Near to tears Elmer was determined now to brazen it out. He would have to run the gauntlet of the hotel lobby and hope there were not too many late nighters left. His pants, he hoped, would be somewhere in the shrubbery. They had to be and he had to find them.

The key to his room at the house where he was staying was in them. And anyhow, he couldn't go there without his pants. The iron lady who ran the joint would never let him in. She'd probably ban him for life.

After ejecting Elmer the girls had called room service and they had stayed up late, Paula and Rose enthralled by Arlene and Laura's tales of Hollywood and the many foibles of men. Consequently they slept late next morning and took breakfast in their room.

Around eleven Herbie rang. "Where are you?" he demanded. "I thought you'd gone home or something."

"What are we doing today?" Rose asked hazily.

"Is Paula there? You and I and Paula and Tom are going to lunch with your friend, the Sheik of Araby."

"Oh, great!" Rose was enthusiastic. She put her hand over the 'phone and told Paula. Paula nodded in agreement. "We'll see you downstairs in half an hour. Got to make ourselves look glamorous for his highness."

"Well, okay," Herbie said. "But not too glamorous. I don't want to end up owning a hundred bloody camels."

Tom and Herbie were in the lobby when Paula and Rose stepped out of the lift. Tom came forward and kissed Paula on the cheek.

"Day off today," he said cheerfully, "and I'd like to spend it all with you - if I may."

"Rosie, you are my posie," Herbie crooned in the exaggerated style of the late Al Jolson. "You are..." He spread his arms. "...my heart's bouquet."

"My goodness!" Paula said. "You two are happy today."

"We're going to have lunch," Herbie announced, "and Bondi is going to honour us with his signature."

"On what?" Rose asked.

Tom smiled. "He's going to foot the bill for our next big feature."

"He's going to pay for everything," Herbie said, with a huge grin. "Underwrite the lot."

But what happened next was something none of them expected and, certainly for Paula and Rose, it turned out to be the most frightening experience of their lives.

Chapter Ten

The sheik had invited them to lunch at the beautifully restored mansion house which he kept as a summer retreat. It was set back from the steadily rising road to Grasse on a wooded hillside with truly magnificent views from its main windows and tiered gardens back to Cannes and the sea. Herbie had hired a chauffeur and a gleaming black Mercedes to take them there in style.

Paula and Rose sat back in the deeply comfortable upholstery, savouring to the full the undeniable luxury of gliding along through a blue sunlit heaven where cypress trees and white, partially hidden villas shimmered in the midday haze of a cloudless sky. Paula was seated between Rose and Tom. Herbie was beside the driver.

In the pale lemon and white sleeveless dress that Rose had persuaded her to buy at a very up-market boutique on the Rue Jean Daumas, Paula felt fresh and at her best and as well now as she would ever be. Buoyed by a sudden exhilarating euphoria, she felt that life was fun and worth living and far from over, a feeling that was reinforced when Tom sought her hand, squeezed it gently and held on to it for the rest of the ride.

A stony-eyed Arab guard scrutinised them, their driver and the interior of the car before nodding to an unseen colleague who activated the electronically controlled gate.

"Bondi's pretty hot on security," Tom commented. "He has to be."

"Why is that?" Paula asked.

"Well, he's not just a playboy sheik," Herbie said from the front seat. "He's pretty high up in the government of his country."

"He was a member of last month's negotiating team with the Israelis," Tom added. "He has to be careful."

"You mean he's in some kind of danger?" Rose asked.

"Well, not exactly," Herbie said. "He just has to be careful, that's all. There are all kinds of nuts about - on both sides."

"He was shot at once," Tom said. "And it wasn't an Israeli. It was someone on his own side."

"It must be very confusing," Paula said.

"It is," Herbie said. "And that's why he's got all these heavies around him."

"Are they armed, do you think?" Rose asked.

"Well," Herbie said, with a laugh, "I don't think it was his lunch that fella was carrying in his armpit."

"How does Bondi know I'm not an Israeli terrorist?" Rose persisted.

"Because he's met you before," Herbie told her, "and he knows you're as daft as a brush."

Rose slapped the back of his bald head lightly and with affection. "Just watch it, slap-head."

A phalanx of tall pines had shielded the house from the road but now the drive curved and the Mercedes came to a halt, crunching the gravel before wide steps that, flanked by rockeries and clumps of blue agapanthi, led up to a white shuttered, burnt orange facade and an imposing, stone pillared entrance.

Tom and Herbie were tie-less and casually dressed in lightweight slacks and linen jackets and with the girls in their summer dresses they seemed oddly out of tune with the two men in suits who lurked by the shrubberies on either side of the house.

One of the men held a walkie-talkie, the other sported a similar but smaller device in his breast pocket. Both wore their coats open and were wearing what looked like shoulder holsters. Both were dark haired with dark eyes and black moustaches, bigger but less handsome replicas of their boss, Bondi.

Paula glanced at Tom and raised her eyebrows minimally as he helped her from the car. Rose stumbled out behind her but Herbie stayed for a moment to reassure the driver who had decided he was not happy to be there and didn't want to wait for them as arranged.

The front door was open in an arched vestibule. The newly arrived guests were ushered through into a square high-ceilinged hall. The sheik came from a side room to greet them, embracing first Herbie and Tom and bowing low to kiss the hands of the ladies.

"I am honoured," he told them gallantly.

"No, no," Herbie disagreed. "We are the ones who are honoured, Bondi. We're delighted to be here."

Paula noticed that the sheik had neither wife nor mistress at his side. He was watched over by male guards and the servants she had glimpsed so far were men. Perhaps he was a bachelor, she thought. Then she decided this was unlikely. He could have a dozen wives at home in his own country and he probably had.

Two anonymous menservants dispensed drinks. Bondi himself drank only water. Rose, despite having been advised by well-meaning friends that a dry martini was not a suitable drink for a hot country, asked for a dry martini. Herbie, who had become a little tense, took a gin and tonic in a determined effort to relax. Tom had a glass of white wine and Paula asked for Perrier.

Tom sipped at his wine sensing, as Herbie had, that the atmosphere had been somewhat strained before their arrival and that total calm had not quite been restored. This was confirmed when Bondi excused himself and went to brief two of his men out in the hall. When he returned he was full of apology.

"I am so sorry," he said. "We had a little disturbance earlier. One of my ... er ... gardeners reported seeing an intruder in the grounds." He shrugged. "I think if this was so the person has gone now. He was said to have climbed a wall but if he did I expect he climbed back again when he saw my dogs."

"Or your minders," Rose said.

Bondi laughed, his dark eyes flashing above the black moustache. "As you imply, my dear, they can appear even more of a deterrent." He extended his arms to both Rose and Paula. "But let us go in to lunch. I am a lucky man to have the pleasure of escorting not one but two lovely ladies."

They were to dine in the smaller of two dining rooms where floor length lace curtains rose and fell with each breath of breeze from two sets of french windows. A sunlit terrace bound by a weathered stone balustrade and flanked by wisteria covered walls drew Paula and she gasped at the view.

She looked out across the wide sweep of country that sloped away to where the town, made miniature by distance, covered the waterfront. Out at sea the dark shape of a tanker lay like a smudge on the pale blur of the horizon. Closer to shore where the iron grey of the water changed to a sparkling blue, a yacht club flotilla circled a tiny bay.

"Just look at that view," she said softly.

Tom was by her side. "I'd rather look at you," he said, with a smile.

The lunch went well. A round table, large enough to be comfortable yet small enough to be friendly, proved more than adequate for the host and his four guests. Conversation came easy and as the meal progressed the sheik and everyone else became more relaxed.

"So," the sheik said, addressing Rose and Paula, "I have beaten you ladies to the post. I am to have the pleasure of financing Mr Kay's new project. I trust you don't resent my intrusion too much?"

"Well," Rose began and Herbie held his breath, wondering what on earth she was about to say, "my only regret is that I might not get to meet the Queen."

"The Queen?" Bondi was intrigued. "Of England?"

"The Queen of England," Rose confirmed. "You see, I'd say there's every possibility that Herbie's next film will be up for a Royal Command performance at the Odeon, Leicester Square." Rose had absolutely no grounds for making such an assertion but this didn't deter her one bit. "And that would mean Her Majesty and Prince Philip would be present. That's why Paula and I were interested in the first place. We just wanted to meet the Queen."

The others were dumbfounded but the sheik was nodding and listening intently. He was either humouring her or he actually believed what she was saying. It was difficult to tell.

"Now it would be you who gets to meet the Queen," Rose went on. "Isn't that right, Herbie?"

Herbie shrugged. "Well, yes. Of course."

"There are more benefits to this movie business than I imagined," the sheik said. "I might even get to sleep with one of those lovely young starlets."

"Starlets?" Rose said scornfully. "I haven't heard that for years. They don't call them that any more."

Her disdain bordered on rudeness. Tactfully, Paula smiled in an effort to lessen the impact. "I suppose it's politically incorrect, as they say."

"Then what do they call them?" the sheik asked politely.

"Actresses?" Paula offered.

Tom shook his head. "No, no. I'm afraid that's out, too, these days. They call themselves 'actors'."

Bondi laughed aloud. "I am not sleeping with any actors."

"Any particular starlet you have in mind, Bondi?" the ever practical Herbie asked, when the laughter subsided.

"Well," the sheik said thoughtfully, "I would certainly like to meet the lovely Nina again."

"Oh no," Rose told him. "Not Nina. Nina is Phillipe's girl friend."

"Then if I am not to sleep with the lovely Nina," he suggested, his dark eyes laughing, "perhaps I might be permitted to sleep with the lovely Rose."

"No chance, sheiky," Rose said at once. "The lovely Rose is with Herb."

"The lovely Paula then?"

"The lovely Paula is with Tom."

"Then who?"

Rose leaned across the table, patted his arm. "Don't worry about it, cock," she consoled him. "If we get as far as a Command Performance we'll fix you up with the Queen. I reckon that old fart Philip is past it nowadays."

The sheik roared with laughter at this and the others joined in, thankful that Rose had talked herself out of a tricky exchange.

"I must confess to you, my dear," the sheik told Rose, as he dabbed his eyes in merriment, "my fantasies are not entirely fanciful and unfulfilled. The lovely Nina was here last night. *All* night."

"The little bitch!" Rose was genuinely shocked as were the others.

Suavely, the sheik turned to Tom and changed the subject. "I understand you have another movie to write before you come to us, Tom."

"That's right," Tom said soberly, restoring a note of calm after all the levity.

Paula watched as the sheik waited for him to elaborate. As always Tom could be relied upon to show just the right amount of deference, respectful but never obsequious, solicitous when necessary but never patronising or insincere.

In a vague way it went through Paula's mind that Herb, the quintessential Cockney, was more like the perceived notion of a typically brash American male than Tom. It also occurred to her that the 'perceived notion' was probably unfair to ninety per cent of American men. British or, rather, English gentlemen, if they had ever been, were no longer the sole arbiters and custodians of good taste.

It was clear the sheik approved of Tom and his manly good manners. And so did Paula. Paula knew now that, like a silly schoolgirl, she was falling in love with him.

"Are we to hear what this movie is about?"

The sheik was simply making polite conversation but for once Tom seemed reluctant to respond. He smiled and then, with no way out, said quietly, "It's a sort of love story."

Showing his tobacco-stained teeth beneath his black moustache, the sheik nodded, willing Tom to continue. But at that moment a long lace curtain fluttered inwards at one of the open french windows and the tall slim figure of a young man appeared.

The young man wore a grey European suit but his head and neck were covered by the kind of snood worn by soldiers and guerrilla fighters in middle east conflicts. The lower half of his face was covered by a silk scarf.

The guests assumed he was one of Bondi's personal bodyguards but the sheik knew at once the man was an intruder. He looked to the door and called out a name but, calmly and carefully, from a shoulder holster, the hooded man drew a Czech-made M52 automatic pistol, attached a silencer and without a moment's hesitation shot dead the guard who came running in.

At the dull thwack-thwack of the muffled bullets everyone realised what was happening and in the ensuing panic Tom pulled Paula from her chair and thrust her under the table. For several seconds chaos reigned, oaths abounded and the sound of running feet echoed on the tiled floor of the hall. The cool young assassin simply took aim and hit Bondi just below the right shoulder.

Blood spurted, soaking though his white shirt and a spreading stain appeared on his ivory linen jacket as he slumped back in his seat. By now two of Bondi's men had returned the gunfire from the door of the dining room. Deafened by the noise, Bondi's luncheon guests were lying on the floor. The assassin, having hit his target, had turned and fled.

"Stay down!" a guard ordered in English and they stayed where they were.

There were more shots now, shots from the terrace to the shrubbery below, and running feet. Dogs barked, excited by the chase, and voices were raised in frantic cries and commands as car tyres screeched, spraying gravel from the drive.

As the action moved away from the dining room, Herbie tried to get to Bondi's side but two of the guards barred his way and it was difficult to see how badly he was hurt. Word had gone out to the emergency services. A doctor and an ambulance crew were on their way. But most of the heated exchanges between Bondi's aides were in the sheik's own language and it was not easy for the guests to follow what was being said.

Clinging to Tom, Paula found she was shaking. He held her gently, calming her, reassuring her. "It's all right," he said softly. "It's over."

At the table Herbie had resumed his seat and was staring into a bowl of flowers. He was concerned for Bondi, of course, but he was also concerned for the effect all this would have on his future plans. If Bondi died there would be no money forthcoming. He would have to find a new backer.

Rose stood behind him, her hands on his shoulders, and murmured consolingly in his ear. He mustn't worry she told him. Things'll work out. You'll see. She knew exactly what was troubling him and she was eager to support him, conscious that his cause was her cause now, as if they were already married.

After what seemed an age but was really no more than fifteen minutes an ambulance raced up the winding drive, killing its siren as it came to a halt, closely followed by two police cars. The large square hall and the small dining room were suddenly flooded with professionals - a doctor, paramedics and policemen.

It was a little before three thirty in the afternoon when the dark eyed young man stepped in from the terrace, shot one man dead with two bullets and hit the sheik in the shoulder with a third. It was almost six thirty in the evening when officialdom had over and over again questioned everyone who was at the scene and everyone who was in the house or its environs at the time of the attack. Everyone, that is, except the assassin who had apparently vanished as swiftly and as stealthily as he had arrived.

If they could, someone remarked, they would take statements from the dogs that were still barking in the bushes. But few of the people present could give worthwhile descriptions of the man. He was young, he was dark, he was around six feet tall. That was about the most anyone could say about him.

"I need a drink," Herbie said at one stage, but the police officer in charge of proceedings forbade anyone to touch the dining table or even the side table where a variety of drinks were set out. Coffee, they were told, was available in the larger dining room. Bondi's housekeeper and two women from the village who assisted her had laid on some light refreshment.

At five thirty Herbie and the others, having supplied every scrap of information about themselves, their work, their relationship with the sheik, their reason for being there, their connection, if any, with the state of Israel and many more answers to these and other sometimes obscure questions, went in search of said refreshment.

But little remained. Locusts in the form of policemen and others had been there before them and some were still standing around, coffee cups and sandwiches in hand. Tom and Herbie sought out the police interpreter. It was time to go, time to be allowed to go. Again they recited their home addresses and the name of the hotel where they could be contacted and at last they were permitted to leave.

"Sank you, sank you for these co-operations," the chief inspector said in his fractured English. "We meet again. Of these I am sure. Sank you, sank you ver' much."

Herbie's hired chauffeur was sitting in the Mercedes out on the drive. He had been grilled relentlessly for almost two hours and he was furious. He was sorry but he would have to bill them for the extra time. He had not expected to have to sit here all afternoon, a prisoner and, from the way the idiot police behaved, some kind of prime suspect when he didn't even know what had happened.

"Yeah, yeah. Fair enough," Herbie agreed, as fed up as the driver. "Let's just go, eh?"

Back at the Carlton news of the shooting had arrived ahead of them and when it became known that Herbie Kay and party had actually been present several journalists and photographers appeared as if from out of the woodwork. Herbie couldn't afford to forego the potential publicity for himself and his future plans and, as if revitalised by the possibilities the situation presented, he settled in a corner of the main bar to hold an impromptu press conference.

Rose, apparently unbowed by the experience, also seemed to have tapped into new springs of energy and enthusiasm and she settled in happily by his side, fielding questions from all angles and enjoying her new role of supportive wife-to-be.

Tom clutched Paula's hand and whispered in her ear, "Let's get outa here!"

Paula nodded and he called to Herbie along the bar, "Catch you later, Herb."

Herbie winked an eye to acknowledge their exit and Rose raised a hand before turning to face yet another barrage of questions.

"Mr Daniels!" One of the scribes attempted to detain Tom but Tom merely smiled and skipped out of his way, taking Paula with him into the mauve glow of the early evening and out on to the Croisette.

CHAPTER ELEVEN

"They're pretty close those two," Paula said, meaning Rose and Herbie.

"Like pages in a book," Tom agreed.

"She's a changed woman," Paula told him. "This holiday has changed her."

"And has it changed you, too?"

"I hope so," she said.

At the corner of the Croisette and the Rue des Serbes there was a sidewalk cafe. It was crowded with minor film people, many of whom Tom seemed to know. He caught a waiter's eye and the waiter held up a hand to indicate he would find them a place.

"If we sit here long enough we might get spotted by some beeg film producer," Tom said facetiously.

"What would he make of us?" Paula asked. "Tarzan and Jane?"

"Hardly," Tom admitted.

"Scarlett and Rhett?"

He shook his head. "After this afternoon, I'd say we'd be better off as Bonnie and Clyde. At least, we'd be armed."

The waiter was inviting them in, directing them to a small wrought iron table with two wrought iron chairs that grated on the pavement as they sat down. After a quick consultation Tom order Perrier for Paula, who absolutely refused to be tempted by anything stronger, and a beer for himself.

Across the road the darkening sea was flecked with gold as the last rays of the sun gradually withdrew from the early evening sky. Paula had picked up her blazer at the hotel and she pulled it on thankfully now.

"What do you want to do about dinner?" Tom asked.

"I really don't know," Paula said. "I think I'm still in a state of shock. I don't know if I've lost my appetite or I could eat a horse."

Tom smiled. "They do a very good horse here. *Cheval en casserole.*"

"No, but seriously..."

He covered her hand with his. "Seriously, darlin'," he said and Paula was charmed by the ease with which the word slipped out. "I understand it affects people in different ways. I read somewhere that soldiers who survive a really fierce battle can sometimes eat enormous meals. I suppose it's a celebration of being alive."

"It was like a dream," Paula said. "As if it wasn't really happening."

"It was happening all right," Tom said. "Any one of us could have been hit." He laughed. "One of the guys who came running in from the hallway had me worried. He was cross-eyed. Just like the guy in the Laurel and Hardy pictures. His first shot hit the chandelier."

"Do you think he'll be all right?" Paula asked, still chilled in retrospect.

"Bondi?" Tom said. "I don't know. He was a pretty awful colour when they carried him out."

"Why would anyone want to kill him? He seems such a nice man. Bit of a roué, I suppose, but apart from that..."

"As far as we know, he is a nice man. But he's from a different world, Paula. They have their own ways. They have their own private wars and vendettas."

"There was something I wanted to ask you," she said. "Just before the man appeared, just before Bondi was shot, he asked about your next film, the script you're due to start work on. You seemed sort of reluctant to tell him anything about it."

"I was," Tom admitted.

"You said it was a love story," Paula prompted.

"It is. It's about Che Guevara, Fidel Castro's side-kick in the Cuban Revolution. Guevara is the hero, the great romantic idealist, probably the world's most famous communist outside of Russia and Chairman Mao. I guess glamorising him isn't going to go down too well with a guy like Bondi. Politically speaking, Bondi is probably several miles to the right of Adolf Hitler."

Paula nodded. "And what's the love story?" she asked, with a smile.

"It seems Che went off on a fund-raising mission to Moscow and he met this beautiful girl, a young Russian journalist - they're always beautiful in books and movies, you'll notice, although I must admit from the shots I've seen this girl wasn't at all bad-looking. Anyhow, she follows him back to Havana and out, eventually, to Bolivia. They have this big romance, they live rough in the hills with the Bolivian army on their tails and they both die in the end."

"How? I mean, how do they die?"

"A bit like Butch Cassidy and Sundance, I suppose. They're hounded and hunted down by hordes of government troops, they're trapped, they face up to impossible odds, they get shot and they die. End of story."

"And it's your job to write the script?"

"A lot of the groundwork has been done," he admitted. "Steve Hogan bought the rights to a magazine story. It's a *true* story, of course. It all actually happened.

The piece was called *Christ in a beret*. You remember all those arty posters of Guevara looking like Christ with his beard and his black beret."

"Should be good," Paula said with enthusiasm.

"Steve's a good director. If he gets a half good script he can usually make something of it."

"So when do you start?"

"Ah!" Tom said. "Well, the plan is that I go off to Bolivia, have a good look around at a place called La Higuera, place where the end came, soak up the atmosphere - probably stay in the capital La Paz. Then get down to work. I reckon I've got until the end of August, then I have to be in LA for Herbie and Rose's wedding."

The waiter hovered, smiling, tray in hand. He was very thin, balding, with bushy black eyebrows and a large black moustache that quivered comically when he spoke. And he was wearing a tight black waistcoat and a white apron, just like a waiter in a silent film.

"You want sam-sing?" he asked. "For dinner, maybe? We haf nize table inside - ver' nize."

"Something light," Paula said.

"We could share a pizza," Tom suggested.

Behind the moustache the waiter's lined face broke into a huge grin. "*Toujours*, we 'ave the bes', the mos' beautiful peeza een these town." He held Paula's chair. "*Et toujours, M'sieur* Daniels, 'e 'as the bes', the mos' beautiful ladies."

"Oh, does he now?" Paula said, eyebrows raised.

"I say sam-sing wrong?" the waiter asked of no one in particular and led them indoors.

Tom suggested a bottle of Chablis but Paula said she would drink no more than half a glass. The last time they were alone together, she reminded him, she had disgraced herself.

"I'd had an awful lot to drink that day," she pleaded in her defence, "and I'm sure you were glad to get rid of me."

"I don't know about that," Tom said. "You were obviously not used to it. I get worried when a girl drinks all day and *doesn't* get drunk."

But Paula wouldn't be tempted further. She was totally in control of her actions, knew exactly what she was doing and was planning to do and she wanted to keep it that way.

Surprisingly, when they left the seafront cafe at around ten, the slightly chilling breeze had dropped and the moonlit night was mild. The prospect of a stroll along the promenade drew them across the still busy Croisette and they went to the rail to look at the sea, ink-black now in the dark but shimmering silver where there was moonlight. There was something sensual in its quietly rhythmic ebb and flow, as if it was dreamily making love to a somnolent shore. Paula found herself drawing closer to Tom, settling neatly like a piece of a puzzle into his arched frame.

"We could go back to my place," Tom suggested, smilingly aware that this sounded like some cheap line from a B-picture. "You could make a proper inspection. I don't suppose you remember much about last time."

Paula laughed aloud and slipped an arm through his. "I do my best not to," she said.

"Well, what do you say? A night cap?"

"I don't wear a night cap."

"But you'll come?"

She nodded. "And I promise, this time I'll be on my

very best behaviour."

"That's no good," he said, with a grin. "That's the last thing I want."

Tom's temporary accommodation was only a short walk up a side road from the Croisette. Paula remembered the girls she had passed on her way back to the hotel the other morning. Two girls, who could have been the same two, were waiting in the shadows. She clung to Tom's arm.

"That's right, honey," one of the girls called out in English. "Hold on to him now."

"She speaks English," Paula said, surprised.

"That's probably because she *is* English." Tom said. "Or from North America. Probably came here with some idea of breaking into the movies and ended up in that racket."

"Does that sort of thing happen a lot?"

"All the time and with some quite young girls, too. I'd say there are just as many pimps here as there are movie producers."

The sight of the street girls plying their age-old trade had put Paula in mind of the modern scourge and the well-publicised dangers of 'unprotected sex' as the newspapers and other media called it. She had quizzed Rose about this earlier. Rose had slept with Herbie and Paula wanted to know what precautions, if any, they had taken. How did she know it was safe to sleep with Herbie? It was a fair question. Herb was an active and long-standing member of the movie-making community which, from all accounts and by reputation, was probably one of the most promiscuous and amoral communities in the world.

"You're wondering if he wore a condom," Rose said,

as forthright and honest as always. "Well, no, he didn't. I asked him and he said he didn't need to. He'd had to have a pretty thorough medical for an insurance policy he'd just taken out and he was 'clean as whistle' - Herbie's words. And furthermore, he said, he'd expected to be. He doesn't sleep around and he had no reason to expect otherwise. But he said if it bothered me he'd wear one - no problem. Seems they have these dispensers in the Gents'. I told him no. I believed him.

"Then he said, 'How about you? How do I know you're not some sex maniac, dragging fellas in off the street?' You don't, I said, and I'm sorry to disappoint you but I'm just a poor, sex-starved widow from South Manchester. I haven't been to bed with a fella since my husband died."

As for Tom, Rose informed her, he and Herb went together for the same medical. You should ask him but I'm sure it's the same with him.

Paula decided she would.

"I haven't been to bed with a woman for a few years now," Tom told her openly. "I was beginning to believe I was past it. I've probably lost the knack anyway - but I used to be pretty good at it." He laughed. "Though I say it myself, I had no problem when I was young. I guess I had more than my fair share. But it hasn't bothered me for a year or two now. Until the other night, that is. If you'd been in a fit state I think we might have. If you'd been willing and sober I'm pretty sure we would have - because I certainly would have. But you weren't and we didn't. And if you're worried about the dangers you needn't be. I just haven't had time for casual relationships."

"Then why now?"

"I don't see this as a casual relationship, Paula. I thought there was a little more to it than that."

Paula recognised the tennis courts and the little church in the Rue du Canada and then they were there. Tom's apartment was on the second floor. She remembered leaving the place in a hurry by the stairs and she began to feel mildly embarrassed as they went up in the lift.

The bright hallway, the carpet with the floral design, everything served to remind her of the way she had felt but this time she was totally sober. She had consumed scarcely anything alcoholic all day - half a glass of wine at the most - and she was glad. The last time she was here she had vowed to herself she would never ever drink too much again.

Tom seemed to sense what was going through her mind. He laughed as he turned the key in the door. "You'll soon find your way around," he said. "Just walk on the ceiling the way you did last time."

"Don't remind me," she warned him, through her teeth.

She examined the bookcase wall as Tom went round switching on discreet lights. The books were mostly thick French encyclopaedias, volumes of French History and a few French classics: Balzac, Flaubert, Stendahl. It was the sort of bookcase that was rarely disturbed, except for dusting. A couple of rows of CDs and cassettes looked more inviting. Tom put on a track and turned the volume down low.

"A drink?" he asked, with another laugh.

"No," she said, "and don't you dare make fun of me. I want to do this with a clear head."

"Do what?"

"This," she said and she took off her blazer and draped it over a chair. Then she removed his jacket, took him by the hand and led him into the bedroom.

He watched with a slightly puzzled smile as she lifted the slim-fitting designer dress she had worn since that morning up and over her head, shook out her hair and stood before him in just her bra and pants. His hands went to the buttons on his shirt but Paula moved them away. That was something she wanted to do herself and, slowly, deftly, she unbuttoned them all until his shirt hung open outside his slacks and she pushed it back from his broad shoulders.

Paula kicked off her shoes and to Tom she seemed even smaller, even more *petite*. He stepped out of his own shoes in response. There was something oddly touching about her slightly comic determination and he knew he shouldn't laugh or even smile. He lowered his head to kiss her but she put a finger to his lips and began to unfasten his belt. The belt relaxed and she unzipped his slacks so that with a little tug from her slender hands they fell to around his ankles. From the living room Frank Sinatra was quietly urging them to take it nice and easy.

Tom looked down at the little heap at his feet then stepped aside and kicked the slacks away. He was down to his briefs now and Paula, in just pants and bra, was standing so close they were almost touching. He waited, half-expecting Paula to change her mind. But Paula didn't hesitate. With both hands behind her back she unhooked her bra and allowed it to swing away and he knew there was no going back.

He put his lips against her neck and along the line of her shoulder then came back to find her mouth and she surrendered herself gladly, willingly, as his hands went inside her pants and gently eased her upwards and towards him.

Their lips were locked now and she pulled down his briefs with a slim cool hand that made him wince with pleasure. Yet there was no sudden madness, no wild abandon. Tom was too expert a lover for that. Instead he lifted her carefully and, as if he was holding some fragile work of art, he carried her to the bed.

Paula drew one leg out of her pants to free herself and shook them down to her ankle and off. Her small body, he found, was soft and supple, yielding to his touch, and with no hard edges. Tom held her close, her head nestled against his chest, her short blonde hair curled in the nape of her neck.

They were locked together now on the bed that was not quite a double, their lips almost touching. Then Paula opened her eyes and Tom opened his mouth to speak but she shook her head, covering his lips with her own, and he accepted that the time for words was over.

Naked, Tom was a bigger man than he appeared when fully dressed. His shoulders were broad and his body was firm with little or no flab anywhere. Regular tennis and a daily swim had seen to that. And he had spent much of his life in sunny climes so that he was tanned in all but the most private places.

Paula felt small and she was conscious, too, that she was no Arlene or Nina with a film star figure. But none of this was of any importance. She was doing what she had decided she would do with the man she wanted to do it with and she was strangely unashamed.

The music in the other room had stopped, a short pause between tracks, and it was quite still in the bedroom, the bed lit only by the pale moonlight from the open window. It was like the moment before some long awaited concert, the moment when the lights go down and an expectant hush falls upon the audience.

Slowly his lips began to move downwards and Paula responded with total abandon, giving herself freely and without restraint. She had started this and now that Tom was in control she was happy, willing him to show her the way. But there was no frenzy, none of the reckless disregard she had feared in the past. It was warm and gentle and controlled and she wanted it to go on forever.

Paula caught her breath and it was then that something extraordinary happened. There was a subtle change, not of pace exactly, more of emphasis. It was as if Tom knew what he'd been searching for and now he'd found it he'd done something, made some slight adjustment that set an irreversible force in motion.

The sensation began down around Paula's toes and crept slowly upwards, higher and higher, until her whole being was engulfed in a hot tide that forced open her mouth in an irrepressible surge of joy. She felt she was about to float away and the feeling of release, a lightness, a weightless freedom sent her into a rapture of total ease and euphoria.

Tom held her tightly, rocking her gently to and fro, holding her head in his hand, and slowly, luxuriously, Paula came down to earth.

They lay back, side by side, and Paula gazed up at the ornate ceiling and the figured coving. It was a cliche, she knew. She'd read it, heard it said in plays and films, but she really did feel more alive now, after what had just happened, than she had ever felt. She reached over and looked down at Tom. He smiled up at her and her short blonde hair fell forward as she kissed him again and again on the lips.

"So how do you do it?" she murmured.

"Do what?"

"What you just did."

"I play it by ear," he said, then they both laughed at the bizarre imagery that, taken literally, so bald a statement conjured up. "Actually," he added, "I thought I'd lost the knack. But with you it all came back."

"I think I love you, Tom Daniels," she told him quietly.

"I believe you," he said, humouring her.

"I do, I do," she protested. "And from now on, whenever I think of tonight - no! Whenever I think of today and everything that's happened, I'll say to myself, 'I love you, Tom Daniels'."

In the living room Sinatra was still bouncing through his long-playing repertoire, inviting them and anyone else who happened to be listening to join him on a trip to Bermuda.

"You may love me now, kid," Tom said, borrowing Humphrey Bogart's voice and his lines from *Casablanca*, "but one day, maybe not today and not tomorrow but soon and for the rest of your life, you'll see that the affairs of two little people don't amount to a hill of beans in..."

Paula pulled the pillow from under his head and hit him with it and they wrestled about the bed until he wrapped his long legs around her and held her in his grip. For a moment she thought they might be about to do it all over again and slowly, sensuously, she began to stroke his naked rear with the flat of her hand. Tom guessed what was in her mind.

"When I was a boy, maybe," he said with a laugh. "But I'm fifty six, for God's sake." He kissed her again to silence her and promised, "But we will."

"Will we?" she asked wistfully.

"I hope so." He eased himself up on one arm to look down at her. "That was one of the nicest things that ever happened to me, Paula," he said quietly, "and you are one of the nicest ladies I have ever known."

"In the Biblical sense?"

"In any sense."

Paula pouted her lips. "Only *one* of?"

He shook his head gravely. "I'm sorry. I tell a lie. You are, without a doubt, the nicest girl I have ever known."

"Good," she laughed and she reached up and rewarded him with a kiss.

Again they lay side by side, watching the slow-moving shadows high on the walls and the ceiling as wisps of cloud drifted across the moon. For now, there was nothing more to say and Paula, quietly content, closed her eyes to savour again the thrill of what had happened.

In recent years, without her consent, her notion of sex had been conditioned and coarsened by all the unnecessary and often sudden and unexpected writhings and groanings on television. It all seemed so base, so basic, animal in fact and at best a little degrading, turning viewers into voyeurs.

But this was not like that. She had never known anything like this. Perhaps it was something Ted could have shown her, given the chance. But she had never given him the chance. A pale shadow of guilt passed over her but she soon dispelled it. No, she decided, this was not something Ted could have done. Ted was kind, courteous and inept. He could never have done what Tom had done. It was a skill, a technique executed with great charm and perhaps only a few men knew how to combine the two.

She thought of young Elmer who wanted to learn from older ladies. Perhaps Elmer's mother was right in her advice. If Elmer's story had any truth in it, that is. It *was* something that had to be learned, a finesse that had to be acquired.

She thought of Elmer again and something Herbie had said. "The kid's right," he said. "Older women are the best and the older the better. They put all they've got into it every time 'cos they always think it could be their last." Rose had walloped him as usual and Paula laughed now and shook quietly at Tom's side.

"So what's funny?" he asked mildly.

"Nothing," she said and she found his hand and placed it high on the inside of her bare leg.

Tom grabbed her around the waist and tickled her ribs until she squealed. "So what's funny?" he demanded.

"Nothing," she said. "I just feel like laughing."

"You were very quiet back there," he said softly.

"I know," she agreed. "But that's me, I suppose. And anyway, I don't believe the ladies of my generation go in for all that *When Harry Met Sally* stuff, moaning and groaning all over the place. It's embarrassing."

"I wouldn't know," he said, with a smile.

"But it was lovely," she told him. "Perfect."

"Good," he said. "Now I want you to stay right there and we'll sleep together, as they say."

"*Sleep* together?" Paula said. "How boring."

"Ah, but who knows what we might get up to? With any luck we may not be able to sleep."

"You want me to stay the night?"

"I want you to stay the night and in the morning we'll take a shower - together, I hope - then we'll have breakfast and when we're ready we'll amble along to the hotel, see what's new."

Paula held up her arms and drew him down into the bed. "Sounds good," she said.

Rose and Herbie were sitting out on the terrace when Paula and Tom arrived. "Well," Herbie said, standing up. "Hello, young lovers."

He drew Tom into the seat beside him and went at once into an earnest discussion about new sources of finance. The sheik's financial activities would obviously be on hold in the aftermath of the attempted assassination and if the worst happened and Bondi didn't pull through then Herbie would have to start all over again in his search for a backer.

Rose tugged Paula down beside her and offered her coffee. "So tell me all about it," she said confidentially. "I want to know all about last night."

"What?" Paula said. "Here?"

"They're not listening," Rose said, meaning Herbie and Tom. "They're too busy working out where their next million is coming from." She leaned closer, lowering her voice. "So how was it?"

"It was ..." Paula said, searching for the right word, "... intoxicating."

"What were you drinking?"

"Nothing alcoholic. Just water."

"You were pissed on Perrier?"

"I was totally sober and I wanted it that way. I wanted to know exactly what was going on."

"Well," Rose said, with a laugh, "whatever went on, it certainly put a sparkle in your eye."

At that moment the young magazine writer Tom had managed to alienate a few days earlier came running out to the terrace. He had something he wanted to tell the world and Herbie Kay's table was as good a place as any. "Hey, Mr Kay!" he gasped. "Guess what!"

"What is it, kid?" Herbie asked. "Your pants on fire?"

"The sheik!" the kid said.

"Is he dead?" Tom asked.

"No, no. They made an arrest. They picked up that French guy. Phillipe something or other."

CHAPTER TWELVE

It was true. Phillipe had been arrested and remanded in custody. But Tom Daniels, who'd had perhaps the best glimpse of the assassin, was certain Phillipe was not the man who shot the sheik. The others were not so sure.

Not only Herbie Kay had been cultivating the sheik. Several people had an interest in his well-being and some of them had gathered in the hotel foyer to discuss this latest development. Word had soon gone round that Phillipe's girlfriend, Nina, had spent the night prior to the attack with the sheik and many were prepared to believe Phillipe was capable of carrying out such an attack in jealousy. But Tom wouldn't hear of it. That was not Phillipe, he insisted. And what's more, he announced, he was going to go along to the prefecture, if that was what they called it, to tell them so.

He was taken quietly aside by the agent, Lefty Lamar, who had been flitting all week, a peripatetic persuader, from one group to another. Among his many clients, Lefty included Arlene and he had corralled Tom now in order to take him into his confidence.

"Trust me," he pleaded. "Don't go to the police just yet. There's a lot riding on this, Tom, and I don't want to blow it. A big story is about to break and it'll do us all, especially Phillipe, a whole lot of good."

"I didn't know you were Phillipe's agent," Tom said.

Lefty winked an eye. "I am now."

Tom didn't have long to wait. As Lefty had promised, a big story was about to break and it broke that evening. Television and the newspapers couldn't get enough of it.

Phillipe had an alibi and it came in the shape of a once famous, soon to be famous again film star. Arlene had emerged from her temporary obscurity to play the role of the year, that of the older woman who has taken the young, handsome actor to her bed and unwittingly freed him from suspicion of attempted murder. Phillipe, she told the world and the local investigating officers, had spent the fateful afternoon in bed with her and could not, therefore, have been at the sheik's house shooting off firearms.

Pictures of Arlene at her most stunningly beautiful were flashed across television screens and would soon appear in newspapers and magazines around the world. Do you believe her? people asked. But it mattered not. Arlene would win over the watchers of television interviews with her frank, open manner and people would want to believe her. Overnight they would love her and overnight they would love her lover. It was the break both she and the unquestionably handsome Phillipe needed.

The story of Nina and the sheik found little or no place, even in the tabloid press. Lefty Lamar saw to that and he played up the romance of the rising young actor and the older but still gorgeous actress to the hilt. Already he spoke of a multi-million dollar movie deal for the two of them. It would be something wonderful. A remake of *Camille*, he hinted. Or something along those lines. A big screen sob-story. They were made for it, made for each other and so he went on and on.

Phillipe was released and soon he seemed to be everywhere, facing photographers with his new soulmate Arlene, their names on everybody's lips. This is great stuff! Rose enthused. The real old razzmatazz!

But do you believe her? Paula asked. So who cares? Herbie argued. It's a great story. And true or not, Tom pointed out, it doesn't matter. There's no way that Phillipe was the guy who shot Bondi.

One of the side benefits of all this was the healing of the rift between Tom and the up-and-coming showbiz magazine. Tom had told Herbie that something big was brewing and Herbie had at once advised him to tip off the magazine's young writer, tell him to stay close to Lefty Lamar. Tom had merely shrugged, refusing to pander, but on his behalf and at Herbie's request Rose had passed on a message to the young journalist, a message purporting to come from Tom.

The young journalist had wasted no time. Lefty Lamar was keen to break the story simultaneously in the States and he was happy to let the kid take the credit. And whether he wanted to be or not Tom Daniels was well and truly back in favour.

Paula had come off her intoxicated high by now and was wondering what direction, if any, her relationship with Tom would take. Was that it? Or would there be more? It was too soon to say and she was glad of the diversion, glad of all the gossip and speculation about Arlene and Phillipe. She was not sure what she wanted to happen next and she wanted time to think about it.

As for Arlene, some believed her, some didn't. But no one seriously believed Phillipe was the would-be assassin. No one, that is, except Marvyn Brodsky, who wanted to believe it and was going round telling anyone who would listen that 'that crazy French bastard' was a jealous, homicidal maniac.

There was a strong suspicion that Brodsky, through

an interpreter, had informed the man from *La Sûreté* of the charge pending in respect of Phillipe's alleged attack on a cameraman in Venice. All this had served to delay Phillipe's release but released he was and Brodsky was furious.

Laura Baker, who was soon to leave for London to begin rehearsals for a stage play, invited Paula, Rose and Arlene - if she can drag herself away from the cameras, she said with a laugh - to a nice quiet little farewell dinner, just the four of them, no men, in La Palme d'Or restaurant at the nearby Hotel Martinez.

Herbie said that was fine by him. He was hoping he might have dinner with a new contact, a film-struck Senator from the Mid-West who was cruising the Med in some billionaire's yacht. He could smell big money, he said, and he wanted Tom to go with him and help him talk about their next project.

Tom said he would do whatever Paula wanted. He had planned to have dinner with her alone, he said, somewhere out on the quay, then take her back to his place. But neither Rose nor Paula wanted to let Laura down. Arlene had already promised Lefty she would do what he wanted - 'talk to the goddam press and get my name in the goddam papers yet again,' as she put it, with her hilarious laugh, as if it was all one big joke - but she would slip away and join them as soon as she could.

Later that day, when they were alone in their room at the Carlton, getting ready to go along the Croisette to the Hotel Martinez, Paula and Rose had a chance to talk things over and assess the week's events.

"I can't believe all that's happened," Rose called from the open door of the bathroom. "How things can change, how your whole life can change in just a few days."

"Nor can I," Paula said and she caught her husband's eye. He seemed to be smiling slightly, watching her from his framed photograph on the dressing table. She looked at him fondly. She still loved him and she always would. That hadn't changed. But he'd gone now and that part of her life was over. After what happened last night she had thought she might feel guilty or ashamed when she faced the photograph again. But she didn't.

"For a couple of weeks, once a year, everyone in this town cons everyone else - or tries to," Rose announced as she came back into the bedroom. "According to Herb, the sheik knew Herb's game from the start. The sheik, you see, was dragging his feet, haggling over contracts and refusing to commit himself, that sort of thing. So Herb introduced a couple of new backers. Us! Angels, they called us. And look at us now." She laughed. "*Fallen* bloody angels. That's us."

"Oh, Rose!" Paula said, glancing at the photograph.

"It was calculated to hurry the sheik up. Herbie knew we weren't loaded. He got that fella Chuck to check up on us. He told me so. And it didn't even occur to him the sheik might do the same. A few 'phone calls to his mates in London and the sheik knew more or less all there is to know about us."

"Wasn't he mad?"

"Who? The sheik? No, it seems he thought it was a great joke. A couple of dumb broads from the north of England, that Chuck fella called us. No, the sheik went along with it. Great sense of humour, the sheik. And the way things have turned out, I'm glad he has. I've half promised him the Queen.

"The thing is," Rose went on, suddenly serious, "we're due home the day after tomorrow and - I don't know how to say this, Paula - but, thanks to you, I've had a wonderful time. I really have. The time of my life."

Paula smiled. "I'm glad. I'm glad you've enjoyed it."

"I've done that all right. But the thing is ..."

"What?"

"I feel sort of guilty. As though I'm letting you down, deserting you, running off with Herb like this."

Paula laughed. "Don't worry about me, Rose. I just hope you know what you're doing. I mean, Herbie's fine. And I'm sure you two will be good for each other. But can he afford you? You and me, love, we've developed expensive tastes."

"We'll be all right," Rose said confidently. "He may not be able to finance his own pictures but he's not short of a few bob."

Paula sensed that something more was troubling Rose. "What is it, Rose? What's the problem?"

Rose looked at her and smiled. "You'll think I'm boring."

"Well," Paula said, "if I do I'll tell you."

Rose was uncharacteristically hesitant. "I'd ... I'd like to be a nicer person."

Paula laughed. "You'd what?"

"I'd like to be a nicer person. I'm serious, Paula. I mean, I've got a sharp tongue. I say things sometimes when I don't mean to."

"You are a nicer person," Paula assured her. "Nicer than most. Believe me. That's why you're my friend. Because you're a nice person. I like you and so does everybody else, everyone who matters."

Rose looked unconvinced.

"You listen to me," Paula ordered. "You are much nicer than those people who go around saying things like 'Shit!' every five minutes and effing this and effing that every other word. They do that because they can't think of anything better. They haven't an ounce of your wit. You are funny, Rose. You make people laugh. You don't have to rely on mindless swear words. And you don't blaspheme. Too many people here go around saying 'Jesus!" and 'Christ!'."

"They don't know any better," Rose offered.

"True," Paula agreed. "They say these things so often they don't even realise they're doing it. And yet it's so offensive. It offends Christians."

"Come on Paula, " Rose reminded her, "you're not exactly a bible-carrying churchgoer."

"That's not the point. It's offensive. It offends me and it offends thousands of others. It's ... It's verbal violence."

"So what brought this on?"

"You did," Paula told her. "Look around, Rose, listen to other people. You don't need to change, they do. You carry on as you are. You can say what you like as long as you don't hurt people and most of the time you don't. You already are a nice person."

Laura was waiting for them in the cocktail lounge at the Hotel Martinez. A man friend, who had enlisted as a temporary escort, ordered drinks for them, waited until the drinks had been delivered, wished them a pleasant evening and an enjoyable meal, kissed Laura lightly on the cheek and left.

"What a nice man," Paula commented.

"He's an old friend," Laura told them.

Then Arlene came running in. "That Lefty Lamar," she said breathlessly, "he'd have me sitting on top of one of the Carlton domes in the altogether if he could."

"Sounds like a good stunt," Laura laughed. "I'll mention it to him."

"You dare!" Arlene warned her. "So what's new on the man front?" She turned to Rose. "Herb treating you right?"

"Like a princess," Rose told her.

"And I can see all's well with you and Tom."

"Does it show?" Paula asked, a little surprised.

"Does from where we're sitting," Laura said. "You're positively blooming."

"So what's next?" Arlene asked exuberantly. "Laura's off to bust the stuffed shirts on Shaftesbury Avenue, I'm going to be a beeg, beeg Hollywood star - again! - and Rosie's getting married. How about you, Paula?"

"Yes," Laura said. "Where do you go from here, Paula?"

"Home, I expect," Paula said. "We've had a good holiday and it's almost over. I have to go home."

"Why?" Arlene demanded. "What have you got there?"

"Not a lot," Rose said bluntly. "Nothing in fact, now that she's on her own. I want her to come to the States with me but she won't."

"I can't go with you and Herbie," Paula protested. "You two are a couple now. You need to be on your own."

"I probably will be," Rose said. "You can bet Herb'll be out wheeling and dealing most days. I'll probably need you."

"Rose is right," Laura said. "Once Herbie gets back to LA she'll not see much of him from breakfast to dinner. Then at dinner, more often than not, she'll be one of a crowd."

"Just make sure he's with you at bedtime," was Arlene's advice. "If you don't see him then you're in trouble."

"If I don't see him then," Rose said, "he's in trouble."

They all laughed and Arlene asked, "How about Tom? What's he doing?"

"He's going to Bolivia," Paula said.

"Bolivia?" Arlene echoed. "I met a guy from Bolivia once. He owned a tin mine. Trouble was, the mine was extinct, washed up. And so was he soon as I found out."

"Why Bolivia?" Laura asked.

"He's going to soak up some atmosphere, get the feel of the place and some background colour for a screenplay he's doing."

"Sounds like a jaunt at the studio's expense," Arlene said, with a laugh. "Good for Tom."

"Why don't you go with him?" Laura suggested.

Paula laughed. "Well, for one thing, he hasn't asked me."

"But would you?" Rose asked. "If he did?"

"I don't know,' Paula said. "I'd have to go home first."

"But why? Why would you?" Rose demanded.

"There are things I have to do."

"What things?" Rose persisted and Paula was relieved when the head waiter intervened to tell Laura that her table was ready.

What followed was one of the most enjoyable evenings Paula and Rose had ever spent. The food and wine were superb and the service was above reproach. Laura, who was obviously known personally to the head waiter, was treated with great charm and even affection. And her guests came in for extra special care and attention.

Arlene and Rose, with more than a little licence, kept up a string of hilarious anecdotes and stories on everything from ageing Lotharios to Hormone Replacement Therapy.

"There was one girl," Arlene told them, "friend of mine, out on holiday in Acapulco. She'd gone in for the patch on the backside. You know, you stick it on and you absorb the stuff through your skin. Well, it seemed to work fine until one night in bed it came off and somehow got stuck to her husband's ass - with dire consequences. I didn't believe her until I met the husband. He had this high-pitched voice and the biggest boobs on the beach."

"It works though," Rose said, when the laughter had subsided. "I mean, look at that Joan Collins."

"She's turned sixty," Paula said, "and she looks about thirty five."

"Ah well," Arlene said, "the thing is with Joan, she keeps this portrait in the attic."

And so it went on. One well-known Hollywood actor was the butt of a number of Arlene's jokes. "He's a real pain in the ass," she confided. "I worked with him once and he kept on and on at me to give him marks out of ten. God, he was so vain! Was he better looking than this guy and that guy. How did I rate him? He insisted, in fact. One to ten. I said nought and he sulked for a fortnight."

"They're vain, all right," Rose said and she recounted the tale of the French actor she and Paula had met at the first party they attended. He was horrible, Paula said. Yeah, Rose agreed, he was going around touching everybody up. He hadn't made a film in years but he told us he was once voted the most handsome man in the whole of France. "He told us he played the lead in his last film," Paula said, taking up the story. "And Rose said, 'What was it? *The Elephant Man*?' "

Encouraged by the response Paula went on to tell the tale of the old man they had met at another party. He was almost totally decrepit himself yet he would insist on patronising all the older ladies present. 'Never mind,' he said at last. 'There's many a good tune played on an old fiddle.' And Rose said, 'But not by you, eh cock? I bet your bow broke years ago.'

"Most men don't know how to do it anyhow," Laura said soberly. "They only think they do."

Rose agreed. "I'm going to have to teach Herb a thing or two."

They all looked at Paula and she laughed in embarrassment. "Don't look at me," she said. "I don't think there's anything I could teach Tom."

"What about Phillipe?" Rose asked Arlene, coming to Paula's rescue. "Did the earth move?"

"No," Arlene laughed. "But the bed did."

Later, as the wine was drained from the last bottle and the waiter offered refills of coffee, Paula was again the focus of attention.

"I propose," Laura announced, a little light-headed by now, "that this conference moves to send Paula to Bolivia with her beloved."

"Hear, hear!" Rose said. "I second that!"

"Carried!" Arlene said.

"What do you say, Paula?" Laura went on. "You can't pass up a chance like this. An exotic holiday with a gorgeous man."

"Tom hasn't asked me," she reminded them.

"You'll never go anywhere," Arlene said, "if you wait for invitations."

"I do have to go home," Paula said firmly. "It's my children. They're expecting me back."

"They don't really want you," Rose told her. "You know they don't. They just want your money. Tell 'em you're skint. See if they want you then."

"Rosie's right," Arlene said. "Tell them you blew it all at blackjack. They won't care if you elope with the milkman then. In fact, they'll be glad to get you off their hands."

From where she was sitting Laura could see the main entrance to the restaurant. She leaned forward to make a warning noise. "O-oh! Here comes trouble!"

Young Elmer, looking bronzed and fit and smartly dressed in a lightweight jacket and tie, his blond hair neatly brushed, approached their table. For once, all four were silenced.

"Ladies," Elmer said, bowing politely. "I've been looking for you and now I've found you - all of you together."

"See you found you trousers, too," Rose said lightly.

He smiled and nodded.

"So what can we do for you, Elmer?" Laura asked. It was her party and she didn't want any trouble.

"I just came to say thank you and I'm sorry."

"You came to thank us?" Arlene queried in surprise.

"I deserved what you did the other night," he told them, "and, as I say, I'm sorry. I apologise. But I'd also like to say thanks because, what happened was, I got a job out of it."

"You did?" Laura was genuinely pleased.

"I got two jobs, in fact," Elmer enthused. "I've been offered a job in publicity. They seemed to think what I was doing was some kind of publicity stunt, running around naked ..." He laughed. "Mr Lamar saw me and he got me fixed up - no problem. But then I told him what had happened and that what I really wanted was to be an actor and he got me an acting job."

"Good old Lefty," Laura said.

"Take it from me, kid," Arlene told him. "He's the best there is. Lefty Lamar has been my agent for ... well, more years than I care to remember."

"They're casting for a movie to be made out in the Pacific and Mr Lamar introduced me to the producer. They reckon I'm just the sort of beef they want."

"Well, that's great, son," Arlene said.

"We're really pleased for you," Laura said.

"And anything must be better than working for that Brodsky," Rose added.

"That's right," Elmer agreed and he told them how he had run to Brodsky's room for help and found the old goat in bed with a couple of kids young enough to be his granddaughters. He said he'd had a mind to report Brodsky to the management for misusing their hotel room and tell the police he was corrupting minors.

"You should have," Laura said.

"You know," Arlene said thoughtfully, "that Brodsky, if you were to write him up as a character in a novel or something folks would say you'd overdone it. Nobody could be that awful. But they'd be wrong, Brodsky *is* that awful."

"Still," Laura said, "you're rid of him now, Elmer."

Elmer nodded. "And it's thanks to you ladies, I don't need him. Thanks again," he said and he bade them good night.

"All's well that ends well," Paula said, as they watched him go.

"Isn't there a play or something by that name?" Rose asked innocently and the hilarity began again.

Chapter Thirteen

In honour of the soon to depart Laura, Freddie Champers had arranged a farewell party to take place the following morning on his accustomed stretch of reserved beach. All his regular friends were invited and in addition to his special guest and, mindful of the attendant publicity, he had expressed the hope that Arlene, too, would be there and that she would be accompanied by Phillipe, the young man the newspapers were calling her toy boy.

Paula and Rose had promised to be down early. Tom and Herbie were waiting in the hotel foyer.

"This could be our last party," Rose said, unusually subdued as they went down in the lift.

"Don't say that," Paula said.

"I mean here," Rose said. "It could be our last party here. At least, until next year. I mean, we're due home tomorrow and I don't want to go. I love this crazy town."

"Did you have a good time last night?" Herbie asked by way of greeting.

"Hilarious," Rose said. "Arlene is a comedian."

"I missed you," Tom told Paula, with a smile.

"She'd have been no good to you, Tom," Rose said. "She was stoned out of her mind."

"I was not!" Paula said indignantly. "Take no notice of her, Tom. I missed you, too."

"Hey!" Rose gave Herbie a dig in the ribs with her elbow. "How about you? Did you miss me?"

"Like a hangover," Herbie said. "Now let's go or we'll miss the party."

Most of the people Paula and Rose had met during the week were already there, along with many they hadn't. Laura was a very popular lady and her friends had turned out to wish her well on her London venture. The champagne, as usual at Freddie's parties, was flowing freely and the cashiered colonel was holding forth. Tom and Paula drifted inadvertently towards him and, without a pause in his flow of words, he acknowledged them with a little wave of his hand.

"Now in the twenties," he was saying, 'they really knew how to enjoy a party."

"Don't say you go that far back," someone interrupted.

"Not quite, dear boy," the colonel said, with a little smile. "Not quite. But on occasions such as this, on an occasion when we must bid farewell, albeit temporarily, to one of our dearest friends, one of the brightest and best-loved of our film stars, there would have been something special. Some grand gesture, some eloquent tribute to our lovely Laura."

"Speeches, you mean?" squeaked a Marilyn Monroe-type *ingénue*.

"No, no, my dear," the colonel said. "What are words? I'm talking about deeds. Actions speak louder than words, my love, as you will doubtless discover."

"What sort of actions?" a cynical, long-nosed press agent enquired nasally.

"Well now," the colonel went on, undaunted, "there was one famous party held just along the coast from here - at Eden Roc, in fact - where a rather well-known lady removed her panties and presented them as a token of farewell to the gentleman who was the guest of honour, one of the male guests jumped into the sea and another - an elderly, highly respected gent, I might add - removed all his clothing and walked slowly and with great dignity back to his hotel."

"Starkers?" a girl asked, wide-eyed.

"Absolutely," the colonel confirmed.

Arlene, listening nearby, her arm dutifully linked to the bulging, muscled arm of her alleged toy boy, took up the challenge at once. With a deft, wriggling motion and a demure raising of each leg in turn - expertly done, as one wag quietly observed - she stepped out of her, very brief, briefs. To the whoops and wolf whistles of the watching men she waved them aloft and demanded they be flown from the nearest beach mast.

Amid cheers and to shouts of encouragement two young men and a smiling waiter each tried in vain to climb the pole. Then, with surprising agility, the superbly fit Phillipe brushed them all aside and hauled himself to the top of the mast where he successfully draped and secured Arlene's briefs to flutter freely in the breeze.

Lefty Lamar looked on, nodding approval. Already he was intent on composing a press release for the gossip columns of the world. 'Brief encounter,' he mused. 'The in-crowd at the lunch-time beach party organised as ever by billionaire Riviera raconteur Freddie "Champers" were delighted when super star Arlene ... et cetera, et cetera.'

But Arlene's bravura performance was soon to be upstaged. No one had jumped into the sea but off to one side an even more remarkable tribute was about to be paid. The retired and permanently scowling producer/director, Jim, and his tall, austere-looking wife, Edina, were quietly emulating the third of the colonel's examples from the Twenties and slowly, systematically, disrobing.

As the various items, neatly folded, accumulated on a small beach table the attention of the crowd was focused in open-mouthed amazement on the two undoubtedly senior citizens. Removing everything but their hats and their beach shoes the strange-looking couple, now even stranger-looking in the nude, bowed majestically to the onlookers. Jim tipped his straw hat and, arm in arm, they made a stately and unhurried exit. Rapturous applause and cries of 'Bravo!' followed them all the way up the steps to the Croisette.

It emerged later that they had crossed the road, causing a near-catastrophic halt in the flow of traffic and an almighty honking of horns, strolled nonchalantly up to the reception desk in the hotel foyer, eliciting more raised eyebrows and dropped jaws, and collected their key. The self-possessed young man on the desk had apparently further enhanced his reputation for cool unflappability by not batting an eyelid.

At Tom's side on the beach, Paula looked as if she had been struck dumb in wonder at what was happening as, drinks in hand, Herbie and Rose joined them. Herbie laughed aloud at the expression on Paula's face. "It's all right, Paula," he said. "Some of these people are quite barmy."

"What do you mean, *some* of them?" Paula asked.

The party went on all morning and well into the afternoon, the noise becoming more and more harsh, the laughter more and more hysterical, as if everyone sensed that the Festival was drawing to a close, that the big party was almost over for another year and that this could be the last opportunity to impress.

Around three o'clock there was a rush for the steps

and a clamour of farewells as Laura's taxi arrived to take her to the airport in Nice.

"I'll be at the Grosvenor House," she told Paula and Rose. "Come and see me when you're in town."

"You're coming to the wedding, aren't you?" Rose demanded.

"Try and stop me," Laura assured her. "To tell you the truth, Rose, the only thing that could stop me is if this goddam play runs through September."

They both knew there was every chance it would but there was not much either could say about that. Laura's professional commitments had to take precedence.

"You'll have to get a stand-in for a couple of nights," Rose said. "You can't miss the wedding of the year."

"We'll see," Laura said, with a smile. "And listen, I'm sure glad we met up. I had a great time and I love you both. Keep in touch, okay?" She hugged Rose and Paula, kissed Tom and Herbie, then said a special goodbye to her friend Arlene. "Take care, huh?" she said, as if to a slightly wayward younger sister. "And I'll see you soon."

There were others standing in line to bid Laura farewell and her departure took some time. Then a traffic policeman moved in to harangue the taxi driver for waiting too long at the kerb-side. Laura climbed in at last and her well-wishers smiled and waved and basked in the warmth her grace and charm had left behind. They lingered in the sunshine, watching until the cab was out of sight in the swarming sheen of vehicles, then went back down the steps to rejoin the party.

On a board-walk an old actor was taking an

enthusiastic young man and a girl in a bikini through some intricate dance steps. Others sighed at the energy of the still lithe old man and helped themselves to more of Freddie's champagne.

The colonel, having taken his fill, was now sound asleep in his deck chair and a small, florid-faced youth with near white hair sat at his feet like a watchful terrier, ready to snap at the heels of anyone who dared to disturb his master.

The party had expanded and as the gatecrashers finally moved in the champagne dried up and those who had actually been invited began to drift away. Even Freddie was no longer there.

"What a swell party this was," Tom said.

"Time to go," Herbie agreed.

With Paula and Rose they climbed the steps and Tom grabbed Paula's hand. "I've been trying to get you alone all day," he said quietly.

"Sounds lovely!" Paula said, a little light-headed.

"I'm serious, Paula. I need to talk to you."

Herbie turned as they emerged on to the Croisette. "What are we doing tonight? It's our last night."

"Something quiet, I hope," Rose said.

Tom and Paula nodded in agreement.

"What do you say we go down to the old port, have a quiet dinner," Herbie went on. "Just the four of us."

"I'm for that," Tom said.

Rose and Paula agreed and that was settled. Across the road at the hotel a tall, dark, fortyish, Arab gentleman was waiting for Herbie. The young man at the desk pointed him out and he rose from his deep armchair to greet them. Paula recognised him at once as one of the men at the sheik's house on the afternoon of the shooting.

Herbie and Tom feared the worst but the envoy, for that was what he was, smiled in reassurance.

"How is the sheik?" Herbie asked, with genuine concern. "Not bad news, I hope?"

"No, no, Meester Kay." His white teeth flashed briefly behind the black moustache all of Bondi's men appeared to wear as if they were standard issue. "My instructions are to inform you that our leader is making excellent progress and that he wishes to honour the agreement he has made with you and your company. The contracts are signed." He tapped his black briefcase. "And my instructions are to deliver them to you personally."

Herbie was clearly delighted and, at Tom's instigation, the others moved away to allow him to conduct his business alone.

Rose took Paula by the arm and to Tom she said, "Tell Herb we'll be down at seven."

"I'll book a table at Louis' for eight o'clock," Tom said. He smiled. "Although knowing Herb he'll want to celebrate now Bondi's checked in."

"We're having a quiet night," Rose insisted. "And you can tell him I said so."

"See you later," Paula said and to her surprise Tom gripped her by the shoulders and kissed her on the lips.

"Seven," he said. "On the dot."

Louis greeted them like long lost friends. "How nize to see you. I 'ave lots of loffly drinks for you an' I am so sad. So soon the beeg feelm show is ovair an'you go 'ome. What will Louis do when you go 'ome?"

"As well as ever, I should think," Herbie said, with a laugh.

The large *patronne* arrived with the outsize, soup-stained menus. "Tonight there is no trouble, eh *M'sieur* 'erbie? No fightin'."

"It wasn't us, *maman*," Herbie told her and he greeted her, as usual, with a kiss on each cheek. "Those people were not in our party."

"Is true, yes?" Louis said. "The boy, 'e is in trouble again, yes? With the guns. You theenk he did this, no?"

"No," Tom said. "We know he didn't."

The *patronne* ignored this. " 'e is no welcome 'ere."

"He's not a bad lad," Herbie said.

Tom shook his head. "Leave it, Herb. Choose the wine."

"Something light," Rose said. "I've still got champagne coming out of my ears."

"I've had quite a lot, too." Paula smiled at Tom. "And I'm not at my best when I drink too much."

Tom held her gaze. "Looks like I'm not going to get you alone, but we're among friends."

Rose raised her eyebrows in expectation. "Are you about to propose, Tom Daniels?"

"Rose!" Paula actually blushed. "Do you mind?"

But Tom merely smiled. "I would," he said, "if I could be sure of the answer."

On which ambiguous note, Herbie said, "We're embarrassing our friends, Rose. I think we better take a walk."

"Sit down," Tom said.

"Yes," Paula said. "Don't be silly."

"I want to ask Paula," Tom went on, "if she'll come with me. To Bolivia. I know it's short notice and all that, but I needed to clear it with Steve Hogan and the Studio." He looked at Paula. "There's no problem,

Paula. The Studio will take care of all our expenses."

"I don't know what to say."

"Think about it," Tom begged her. "*Please.*"

"What's there to think about?" Rose demanded. "Just say yes or nod your head - anything. You can't miss a chance like this."

"Well," Tom said. "It's not exactly a holiday. I'll be working ..."

"And what would I be doing?" Paula asked.

"Officially, you'd be working too. You'd be my personal assistant. On the payroll, of course."

Herbie laughed. "PA to a screen-writer? That's a new one."

"Okay," Tom said. "Anything. Secretary, aide-de-camp, collaborator, you name it."

"Girlfriend?" Herbie suggested.

"The man's offering her a job," Rose told him. "A proper job."

"I can type," Paula announced proudly. "I haven't worked or, rather, I haven't had a paid job since I was married. But I was a pretty good secretary once, though I say it myself."

"There you go then," Tom said, delighted. "We leave next Wednesday. From Madrid. I thought we could drive down to Madrid, have a week-end there ..."

"Hey!" Paula called a halt. "It's not that simple, I'm afraid. I have to go home tomorrow. People are expecting me. I have things to do."

"Okay," Tom said. "That's fine. You go home tomorrow with Rose and Herb then you fly to Madrid on Sunday. That'll give you all day Saturday to sort things out at home and we'll still have time to do the Prado."

"She has no excuse, Tom," Rose told him. "She has two daughters at home and they're both old enough to take care of themselves. One's married with a couple of kids, for God's sake!"

"Let me think about it," Paula pleaded.

Tom nodded. "Sure. I just didn't think. I'm sorry to spring it on you like this."

"You got plenty of time," Herbie said, with a laugh. "You got at least until lunch time tomorrow. Our flight leaves at one thirty."

Rose told Paula she wanted to spend the last night in Cannes with Herb. If Paula wanted to invite Tom back then the way was clear. Paula did and Tom accepted.

The single bed was even narrower than the bed at Tom's place but it made little difference to their enjoyment. Paula made the running, undressing him slowly and drawing him between the sheets. But when the time came Tom as before took over and, with several new moves that first shocked then delighted, brought her again to a searing climax.

"How do you do that?" she murmured dreamily as she stretched naked across him.

He smiled, that slow smile that always meant that a quiet joke, some side-stepping one-liner was on the way.

"No, Tom," she said, her bare leg straddling his chest, her eyes suddenly wide open. "*Tell* me."

"There's nothing to tell," he said, both arms around her. "If you say it's a technique then you reduce it to something mechanical and it isn't that. It's a combination of things. The right place, the right mood, the right girl.

It has to be the right girl." She struggled to free herself but he tightened his grip. "And there's something else. Something it's impossible to define. W C Fields used to tell this story about how, when he was young and working as a juggler in vaudeville, he read a book about juggling. It sort of analysed how miraculous a juggler's co-ordination is, how a juggler has to think of so many different things at once, dancing with danger as he does. He was fascinated, sort of filled with wonder at how clever he must be. Then the next time he went on stage he dropped everything."

Paula gazed at him in mock awe and amazement. "You mean you can do that - what you just did - and juggle at the same time?"

And so they wrestled and fooled around like a couple of teenagers who have just discovered the joy of grappling naked with a member of the opposite sex.

"You have to come with me," Tom said at last, out of breath now as he gripped her wrists and pinned her to the bed. "I don't want to go to Bolivia. Not without you."

Next morning in the foyer, packed and ready to leave for the airport, Rose said, "I think you should go, Paula, and so does Herb."

"I have to go home," Paula insisted. "You know that."

"But you don't have to *stay* home," Rose argued. "And anyway, you can't stay home. You haven't got a cleaner."

Tom accompanied them to the airport in Nice. Resisting the efforts of porters to wrest it from him, he carried Paula's suitcase to the check-in. At the gate to the departure lounge he said goodbye, see you in LA to Rose and Herbie, and held Paula back.

"In Bolivia," he said, "the tin mines are all closed today and the flags on all the public buildings are at half-mast because they heard you might not be coming."

"Tom," Paula said. "I'd like to come. I'd love to come."

"But what?" he demanded. "What have you got to lose?"

"I don't know."

He held her arms. "Look," he said. "I didn't ask you to marry me because I didn't want to force you into something you're not ready for. But if that's what it takes ..."

She shook her head and put her fingers to his lips. "No, Tom, not yet."

"Herb asked Rose," he said.

Paula smiled. "Knowing Rose," she said. "I should think she probably asked Herb."

But Tom was serious. "It's up to you, Paula. Whichever way we do it, I want us to spend the rest of our lives together."

Paula couldn't think straight and she had to go. But she didn't want to leave him like this. "I need time ..."

He nodded, resigned to losing her. For now, at least.

Then suddenly she reached up and kissed him lightly on the lips and, without looking back, she turned and ran.

Chapter Fourteen

It was raining in Manchester. Rose's son, Phil, had come to pick them up from the airport. He dropped Paula off first. Paula's younger daughter, Pam, was waiting for her, standing in the front porch out of the rain and wondering who the plump man with the bald head was. Herbie was helping Paula with her suitcase. Phil took it from him and carried it as far as the front door. Then, as the downpour increased, he ran back to the car and in a flurry of waving hands drove off.

Paula kissed her daughter in greeting and looked around at the familiar hallway. She hadn't realised it had become a little shabby of late but she noticed it now. She glanced in the living room then went down the hall to the kitchen where a small pile of unopened mail awaited her return.

"So how is everyone?"

"Fine," Pam reported, putting the kettle on.

"Children all right?"

"Oh yes, I think so. Susie caught chicken-pox but so did half the junior school."

Paula was skimming through her post. "I've won fifty pounds on the premium bonds."

"Good," Pam said. "We had three numbers on the lottery first week you were away. We won ten pounds - so you don't have to pay for a couple of weeks."

Pam ran a syndicate with her mother and her sister and she was always complaining that her sister rarely paid up. 'She'd want her share if we won the jackpot though,' was her familiar cry.

"Your luck must be in, mum."

Paula looked up, her eyes shining. "Oh yes," she agreed. "I think it is. It really is."

Pam paused, empty teapot in hand, a little surprised at the unexpectedly enthusiastic response. "You had a good holiday then?"

"Oh yes. We did. We had a lovely holiday."

"I must say, we were a bit surprised when we got your card. South of France in May. Was it warm enough?"

"I think we were lucky with the weather. It was lovely."

"Good," Pam said. "But you're glad to be back."

It was a statement not a question and Paula was glad it didn't require an answer.

"Kettle's boiling," Pam said.

"I won't be a minute." Paula went out to take off her coat, change her shoes, go up to the bathroom and revert to her former self.

On her way back she looked in again at the living room. Barely lived in, it seemed, since her departure. The piano looked lonely and abandoned. She and Ted had bought that piano at a time when they could ill afford it. Both girls had wanted piano lessons simply because their friends were having piano lessons. They had passed all the grades yet neither could play much or even tried now.

She looked through the patio window at the large rear garden. Hedges trimmed, grass cut. The gardener, Joe, had been and done his weekly job. And a pretty basic job it was, too. But then she wouldn't let him loose on the borders. Anything that wasn't obviously in bloom was, in Joe's estimation, a weed and was instantly dug up and discarded.

She thought of all the hours she had spent here, enclosed by these four walls. The large, comfortable sofa, the two easy chairs. She smiled at the word 'comfortable'. She had been comfortable here. 'Comfortably off,' as people say. But now she didn't want to feel comfortable and 'settled' and resigned to a predictable steady decline. She was brimming over with a new, exuberant energy. She wasn't dead yet and she didn't want to lie down. She laughed. Not on her own, anyway!

A shaft of sunlight through the momentarily stalled rain exposed a film of dust on the television screen. The events of the past thirty years had passed through that and their previous TV sets, washing over them in quickly forgotten waves of information and what passed for entertainment. Rose rarely watched television. It can become a substitute for living, she said, if you let it.

"Mum!"

"Coming," she called and as she passed through the hall on her way to the kitchen there was an insistent tap-tapping at the front door followed by the doorbell. It was the children with their mother Alison, Paula's elder daughter. Paula hoped Geoffrey wasn't with them and fortunately he wasn't. She wasn't in the mood for Geoffrey.

Alison's greeting was as theatrical as ever and her two children swarmed around Paula's legs. All three wanted to be heard at once as she led them through to the kitchen.

"I'll have a cup of tea, Pam," Alison said.

"What did you bring us, gran'ma?" asked one of the children and the other joined in.

"Be quiet, you two," their mother scolded. "Gran'ma

may not have brought you anything."

"In that green bag in the hall," Paula told them and they dashed off to investigate.

"The Cannes Film Festival," Alison said accusingly. "Did you meet lots of famous film stars?"

"Well," Paula said. "Some."

"Who?" Pam demanded. "Who did you meet?"

"I'll tell you about it later," she said, feeling strangely reluctant to tell them about Laura and Arlene, about whom she had met and some of the many things that had happened in the past two weeks.

The telephone burred on the kitchen wall and Pam picked it up. "Hi! Did you have a good time? Yes, I bet! Here's Mum." She held the receiver up with one hand over the mouthpiece. "It's second-hand Rose."

Her mother looked at her askance and took the 'phone. "Hello, Rose. Everything all right? Yes, I'd love to. When? Tomorrow lunch? I think so. Yes. Speak to you later."

"She sounds full of beans," Pam said.

"She wants me to have lunch with her tomorrow."

"Lunch?" Alison wrinkled her nose. "With Rose?"

Pam had sensed there was something different about Rose, some subtle change had taken place. "Who was that man she was with? The Bob Hoskins look-alike."

Paula smiled. "That was Herbie. Mr Herbert H. Kay."

"Herbie?" they echoed.

"He's a film producer."

"What was he doing with Rose?" Alison asked, her cup halted half-way to her lips.

"He's her fiancé," Paula said, enjoying the exchange. "They're going to be married."

"Mum," Pam said in disbelief.

"It's true," Paula said. "They're going to be married in September in LA."

"LA?" they echoed again, taken aback at their mother's air of sophistication.

"Los Angeles," Paula said. "I'm her chief bridesmaid."

The telephone rang again and Pam picked it up.

"Paula baby." It was Herbie.

"Hold on a moment, please." Pam looked at her mother. "Paula baby."

Paula smiled and took the 'phone. "Hello, Herb."

Alison and Pam silenced the children to listen in awe.

"Fine," Paula said. "See you then." She replaced the receiver and smiled at her open-mouthed daughters. "It was Herb. Mr Herbert H.Kay. He's booked a table at the Belfry tomorrow. Twelve thirty for one. Then he and Rose are going down to London to see Herb's family before flying off to the States."

"Mum," Pam said. "Will you sit down for a minute, please? Tell us what on earth is going on."

Rose and Herbie were in the cocktail bar when Paula arrived and they were obviously in good spirits.

"Paula!" Herbie kissed her on the cheek and asked what she would have.

"Perrier, please," she said, but then she changed her mind. "No, I won't. I'll have a glass of dry white."

"So have you spoken to Tom yet?" Rose asked.

"Give me a chance," Paula said.

"You must 'phone him," Rose urged. "Tell him you'll go with him. The longer you leave it the harder it gets."

"I have to break it to the girls - gently."

"Why? They'll only try to talk you out of it."

"What did your Phil say?"

"Phil? He was thrilled to bits. He really was. He likes Herb and Herb likes him. In fact, I think Phil fancies LA more than I do. Herb has invited him to come over and stay with us. Stay as long as you like, he said. Trouble is, he doesn't know our Phil. He'll come over all right and if he can get himself fixed up with a job in the film business he will." She laughed. "We'll never get rid of him."

Herbie came back from the bar. "I'm relying on you, you know that, don't you, Paula?"

"To do what?"

"To bring Tom back from Bolivia. I want you to go out there, stay with him, make sure he gets down to work and finishes off this job for Steve Hogan. Then you can deliver him to me in LA. We can't afford any delays and I'm not talking about the wedding."

"He gave me a copy of the story on which his screenplay is to be based," Paula said, feeling very professional, "and a book about Che Guevara. I've got some reading to do."

"That's my girl," Herbie said. "You'll enjoy it. Tom's a fast worker when he gets started." He smiled. "I'm just a bit worried you two might get to like the South American way and get lost somewhere. We want you in LA early September, end of August if poss. And don't you forget it."

"She hasn't decided she's going yet," Rose said.

"Of course she's going."

"It's a big step," Paula said lamely. "I mean, it's on the other side of the world."

"The world's a small place nowadays, Paula,"

Herbie said. "If you don't like Bolivia you can be on a 'plane and home in a day."

"It's such short notice."

"Nah!" Herbie told her. "Tom's not going yet. He's going back to LA first."

"But I thought ..."

"Changed his plans. He was just trying to stampede you into making up your mind. I mean, you have to have jabs and things for a trip like that. He's going back to LA. Got some work with Hogan at the studio first. Then he's going out there in a week or two. And he's hoping to take you with him."

"How do you know all this?"

"I spoke to him this morning."

"You did? How is he?"

"He's fine." Herbie laughed. "Same as he was yesterday, I guess. And he'll be even better if he gets a call from you."

Still Paula wouldn't commit herself. "I have a few things I need to sort out."

"Like getting the groceries," Rose said scornfully, "and mooching about Marks and Spencer's and minding the kids and watching television and the Antique bloody Road Show."

"Your table is ready, sir," the smiling head waiter informed Herbie.

Herbie stood up. "Come, ladies, let us eat, drink and be merry for tomorrow - who knows?"

"We die, presumably," Paula said.

"So who cares?" Rose added, with a laugh. "So long as it's not in bloody Sainsbury's."

"The thing is," Alison said, "Geoffrey reckons that now

the children are both at junior school I could get my old job back."

"Full time?" Pam asked.

"Well, yes, I'd be home by six, six-thirty ..." She looked at Paula. "...and we thought perhaps Mum could pick them up and give them their tea."

"I've been offered a job," Paula said quietly.

Both girls looked at her as if she had said she was about to take up hand-gliding. "*You*?"

"Yes, *me*," she said. "Why not me?"

"Doing what?" Pam asked.

"Personal Assistant to a top screen-writer."

"A screen-writer? Where?"

"Bolivia," she said, as if Bolivia was just down the road.

"Mum!" Alison said. "I'm serious. I'm sure I can get my old job back."

"And I'm serious too. I've been offered a job with a film studio. I'd be going to Bolivia for a few weeks then back to the States."

"The States?" they said simultaneously.

"Hollywood, to be exact. I'd be working in Hollywood for a time and I have to be in Los Angeles anyway in September for Rose's wedding."

"Who is this screen-writer?" Pam asked.

"His name is Tom Daniels and he has some pretty good credits to his name."

"But you have no qualifications."

Paula smiled. "Tom seems to think I have."

Alison look speechless but Pam, who had always been rather more perceptive than her sister, asked, "Who is he, Mum? How did you come to meet him?"

"I met him at the hotel in Cannes."

"But what about us?" Alison had found her voice.

"Well, you're a married woman with a husband and two children, Alison. I'm sure you can take care of yourself. And Pam, well you are all right here. You're always talking about finding a flat, wanting your own space. You can have the house to yourself for a while."

"And where would *you* live?" Pam asked.

"In America with Rose - until she's married."

"Well, I think you're mad," Alison told her. "And Geoffrey will think so, too."

Two days later Paula was on the Inter-City train speeding south. Herbie and Rose were staying at the Waldorf and Rose was coming to meet her at Euston.

Speeding by the fields of middle England, Paula glowed with a mixture of excitement, anticipation and just a hint of trepidation. The crazy life was to go on for a little longer. A few days in London, then off to LA and who knows what? It was probably, she knew, no more than an extended flight of fancy. A trip to the moon on gossamer wings. But she didn't care. She was alive, she was free and she had no feelings of guilt.

Her younger daughter Pam had seen the advantages of getting rid of her mother for a while and had given her blessing. Her elder daughter Alison, through her husband Geoffrey, had seen only the disadvantages and had given her a month at the most before she came running home, chastened and wiser.

As the train drew in Rose was waiting on the platform. She greeted Paula with a hug and, as if holding back some big surprise, led her up to the main concourse.

Paula saw Herbie first. He was standing before the

giant arrivals and departures board, an unlit cigar between his teeth. Then she saw Tom, his dark eyes smiling. Tom hadn't wasted any time. A 'phone call from Herbie and he'd jumped on the first available flight from Nice.

She dropped her suitcase and ran to meet him and Tom swept her up into his arms. Rose laughed and Herbie flourished his cigar. "Just look at that," he said. "Isn't that beautiful? Straight out of one of those corny Hollywood movies!"

Then they all laughed and arm in arm, the four of them - Herbie, Rose, Paula and Tom - set off in search of a taxi.